P9-DXE-588

One SIMPLE WISH

Katy Lee

Annie's®

AnniesFiction.com

One Simple Wish
Copyright © 2017, 2021 Annie's.

All rights reserved. No part of this publication may be reproduced, stored in a retrieval system, or transmitted in any form or by any means—electronic, mechanical, photocopying, recording or otherwise—without the prior written permission of the publisher. The only exception is brief quotations in printed reviews. For information address Annie's, 306 East Parr Road, Berne, Indiana 46711-1138.

The characters and events in this book are fictional, and any resemblance to actual persons or events is coincidental.

Library of Congress-in-Publication Data
One Simple Wish/ by Katy Lee
p. cm.
I. Title
                            2017947228

AnniesFiction.com
(800) 282-6643
Hearts of Amish Country™
Series Creator: Shari Lohner
Series Editor: Janice Tate

10 11 12 13 14 | Printed in China | 9 8 7 6 5 4

Weeping may endure for a night, but joy comes in the morning. *(Psalm 30:5)*

"Dear *Gött*, it's morning, so why can't I cease this blubbering?" Eva Stoltz shook the reins to her bay mare, Keepsake, and sniffed loudly in the cold, dark December morning. The sweet aroma of fresh bread met her nose as Keepsake took the turn onto the empty village street.

The bread was baked each morning, a symbol of a new day, another chance at life. As a baker at her aunts' Amish bakery, Eva typically took joy in giving the residents of Blossom Creek, Ohio, their daily fresh start.

But today she was in need of her own fresh start, something other than working at the bakery for the rest of her life. Something that helped her forget what day it was. Something that would make her forget about Daniel and his bride.

Another batch of tears fell from Eva's eyes.

Keepsake pulled the buggy through the light snow, her footing sure even without direction from her woeful driver. The wheels creaked as the horse took the turn and ambled up alongside the white, two-story bakery storefront, passed through the narrow driveway to the parking lot behind, then continued on into the barn, where she stopped with a nicker.

Home away from home for them both.

Aunt Louisa and Aunt Rhoda were her *Daed*'s sisters and her two spiritual mothers. Though she loved her *Mamm* very much, it was these two women who could ease the pain in Eva's heart today.

She hoped so, anyway.

Please, Gött, let this grief end!

Eva went through the motions of stabling Keepsake, which gave her time to dry her eyes.

But she knew that her aunts could not be deceived. Neither woman had ever married, but each had just as much intuition as any *Mudder* with a buggy full of *Bobblin*. The Amish in their district would say even more so. Louisa and Rhoda had a keen sense that kept them a step ahead of the people around them, including those in far-off communities. Whether in Blossom Creek or Lancaster, Pennsylvania, nothing escaped their notice. Eva had no hope that her dried tears would cover up anything this morning.

And sure enough . . .

"*Ach*, Eva, again with the tears. The grief has not lessened?" Louisa's plump hands reached for Eva's cloak as she shut the bakery's door on the swirling snow.

"I'm sorry I'm late. I could smell the bread baking at the end of the street. Thank you for starting it for me. I'll get to peeling the apples right away."

"No, you will not. There's no sense in pretending all is well with your soul. Not with us, child." Louisa shook the dusting of snowflakes off Eva's woolen garment and hung it on the wall peg.

Eva ignored the term *child* and untied her traveling bonnet, joining it with the cloak on the wall. Even though she was twenty-three, her aunts still referred to her as a child. But what could Eva expect when she showed up on their doorstep blubbering like one? "You're right. I didn't mean to start again."

Aunt Rhoda carried Eva's baking apron to her. "Yesterday you seemed so much like your cheerful self. We had hopes—"

"Today's the day," Eva responded, cutting her off.

It was all she had to say.

"Ach," Louisa said again, pulling Eva close. "Did you think we did not know this? We had simply been hoping this day would pass like any other for you."

Eva sighed as she leaned into the embrace. She closed her eyes and allowed the warm, sweet smells of the bakery that she always associated with her aunts to seep in. Eva couldn't carry on like this all morning. If it had been anyone else besides Rhoda and Louisa, she would have hidden away her heartache for a private time. But everyone in the room knew the truth, especially with the calendar on the wall displaying the single scratched-out item.

Today should have been Eva's wedding day.

The date had been chosen a month ago, but only a handful of people knew. Eva and Daniel had never published their announcement in the church. Daniel had expressed a need for waiting until his Mamm felt better after a prolonged illness during the last harvest.

Eva had believed him.

And why not? He'd courted her in his open buggy for months. Whispers and giggles went out in the community. The announcement was expected any day. Eva could hardly sleep in anticipation of joining Daniel at the church service for the bishop's instruction and blessing. Her aunts had scolded her for slacking at the bakery in her sleep-deprived state, but they had also teased her kindly. The truth had come as a shock to all.

All along Daniel had wanted to marry another woman, and he'd been waiting for her to say yes.

Two weeks ago, a letter had arrived at the bakery from Daniel. All it said was that he was going to Lancaster to marry his bride, and someday he hoped Eva would understand.

Understand?

Understand that Daniel had been thinking of another woman while she sat beside him in his buggy? Understand that he had gazed into her eyes and thought of another's?

Eva could only understand that he found her lacking.

She stepped away from Aunt Louisa and slipped into her baking apron. It was time to get back to work. It was time to accept that she would be an old maid like her aunts. As Christmas approached in three weeks, Eva's marriageable years had come to an end.

Two sets of kind blue eyes watched Eva intently fix her white *Kapp* over her reddish-blonde hair. Their own graying hair had matched hers in their youth, but they both still wore their long strands parted in the middle and pulled back into tight buns. For a baker, the tighter the better. Nothing loose to conflict with their livelihood. And now it would be Eva's livelihood as well.

The bakery was split by swinging doors, with the store and café in the front and the kitchen in the back. A staircase on the rear interior wall led to a hallway and two apartments upstairs. Louisa and Rhoda lived in one, and the other was rented out. Additionally, there was a stairway outside the back of the bakery that gave a private entrance to the rental apartment. Eva wondered if she should plan to move in permanently. She might as well embrace her future.

"The life of a baker in the family business is my place now. It is Gött's will."

"Are you sure about that?" Louisa crossed her arms as if to show her objection.

Eva couldn't verbalize a confirmation, so she opened the apple bin and pulled the hem of her apron up, forming a pocket to hold the fruit. "It is a good and noble profession," she said. She would learn to be content.

"But what does your heart desire?" Rhoda asked from behind her.

Eva turned around so quickly that three apples escaped her apron and rolled to the corners of the room, one bumping against a stool. "What my heart desires doesn't matter. It's what Gött wants for me that is my desire. You know that. You taught me . . ." Eva's voice trailed off when she noticed Rhoda holding a small box with a red ribbon around it.

A present?

"What is that for?" she asked.

The two sisters shared a secretive smile, and then Louisa said, "We want to give you your Christmas present."

Eva let the apples roll onto the counter. "But it's not Christmas yet." She eyed the gift in her aunt's palm. The box was carved with some sort of design around its sides. A simple one, just enough not to be overly decorative, but pleasing. *Why?* Because she cried out for pity?

Guilt filled Eva, and her eyes welled up again. "*Ich liebe dich.* I do. I love you so much, but—"

"But you don't want to end up like us."

Was she that transparent? Dread moved her feet forward. "That's not what I was going to say at all! I was going to say that I don't deserve it. I would consider it a blessing from Gött to be like you both—strong and kind. You are pillars in the community, respected and loved by all because of your wisdom."

The two women laughed robustly.

Louisa elbowed her sister. "A nice way of saying 'the old maids of the village.' We live this life by choice, content to be companions for each other instead of wives and mothers. Also our choice because it was Gött's will for us. But we know Gött has different plans for you. Eva, you have much love to give. Your heart is full of charity for each person who walks through these doors. Perhaps Gött wants to do something with that love. That is why we want to give you this."

Rhoda nodded for her to take it.

Eva was surprised by how light the box felt in her hand. She untied the bow and let the silky fabric strings hang down as she lifted the hinged lid.

Empty.

She looked to them for an explanation.

"The box is the gift," Rhoda confirmed. "You have to fill it with whatever is in your heart."

"With what?" Eva asked in confusion.

"Your heart's desire. Write it down and put it in the box. Let this be a time between you and Gött. Share the desire of your heart with Him."

"Aunts, I'm thankful for this thoughtful gift, but I'm twenty-three. The wedding season is over. I will have no more opportunities to marry. It's too late to be courted, *if* there was anyone who wanted to court me. You must see how silly this is."

"Is marriage the desire of your heart?" Rhoda asked simply, a ghost of a smile on her thin lips.

Her question caught Eva off guard. The word *yes* stalled on the tip of her tongue.

Her aunts waited quietly for her answer—as did the empty box.

Slowly Eva closed the lid, knowing this couldn't be a casual response. Taking this lightly would only set her up for more heartache. "Would it be okay if I took a few minutes alone?"

Louisa clasped her hands together, her smile reaching her eyes.

Rhoda waved her hands at Eva to move her along. "Go upstairs. The tenant moved out, so the apartment is all yours for reflection this morning. We will pray that His will for your life will become clear. We'll also start the pastry dough, so don't rush. Now go." Rhoda shooed her in the direction of the back stairs.

Eva placed a quick kiss on each of their cheeks, grabbed some paper and a pencil off the sideboard, then rushed to the stairs with her prayer box. She ascended the steps for her time alone with Gött to find her heart's desire. With each step, she prayed for a revelation.

"Don't get comfortable up there!" Rhoda called from below. "That's not your future, Eva."

Eva smiled at her aunt's words. They really did see right through her. This gave Eva hope that they were right, that Gött had a different plan for her life.

At the top of the staircase, Eva entered the private quarters, closed the door, and took in the quiet apartment. With its handmade furniture and humble decor, the living space resembled a good, plain Amish home. A woodstove nestled in one corner of the parlor portion of the kitchen sat cold, but the heat from the ovens below offered warmth.

As Eva walked through the sparse rooms to the small bedroom, she had to admit the place would be a nice home—for someone other than her. An Amish traveler would feel welcome here. Before Eva realized she was doing it, she lifted up a few thoughts about the future tenant. It was easy to pray for someone else, even someone she didn't know. Asking Gött for something for herself felt unnatural, selfish. So for now, she asked His blessing for the new tenant.

Prayers for safety, for peace, for wisdom filtered through her mind and speech. She knelt beside the bed, ready to begin prayers for herself.

Only her words drifted back to the traveler.

More prayers for someone I do not know? She wondered why her mind had gone in this direction, but as she spoke the words aloud, she knew they were right to say.

"I ask for Gött's hand to guide this traveler, not only from harm but into a life of honor and integrity."

Eva reasoned she asked these things because her aunts should have a worthy and respectable tenant, but the flutter of her heart told her this supplication was for so much more.

My heart's desire is for someone I've never met? The absurdity nearly made her laugh—until she glanced at the prayer box on the bed in front of her.

Eva lifted the lid reverently. She prayed with fervor for this man of compassion and fairness. The words *honor* and *faithfulness* and *honesty* sprang from her lips, and before she knew it, thirty minutes went by. Maybe it was because of Daniel's lies and rejection, but Eva took the pencil and paper and wrote one sentence:

I wish for this honorable man to be mine.

She folded the paper and slipped it inside, closing the lid in silence.

Clarity came through. Her heart desired a man with these qualities and values. Not just any marriage but a virtuous one.

"I was so ready to settle, Lord, but You showed me a better way. You showed me what You desire for me, and if this is Your will, let it be so."

A giggle from behind Eva rudely interrupted her moment of entreaty. Eva whirled around to find her younger sister emerging from the closet.

"How long have you been in there?" Eva demanded, now on her feet.

"I was out late last night, so I stayed here," Annie admitted. "I snuck into the closet when I heard you coming up. I thought you were one of the aunts."

"Mamm and Daed don't know you're here?"

"It's expected." Annie's simple response explained it all. At seventeen, she was still in her *Rumspringa*. Her sister had another year to run free before she would need to make the decision to remain Amish and join the church—or go out into the *Englisch* world. Eva knew her parents would turn a blind eye when their daughter snuck back into the house this morning.

Annie flashed a mobile phone in Eva's face.

Eva didn't think they would turn a blind eye to that. "Where did *that* come from?"

"I bought it and sewed a secret pocket into my dress." Annie revealed the phone's hiding place, an opening in her pocket seams.

"Annie, you shouldn't—"

"You're just jealous because you gave up your Rumspringa to make Daniel King think you were marriage-worthy. You wasted years waiting for him."

Eva winced at Annie's crass remarks. Did her little sister think she lacked discretion? Did she come off as wanton? What was the rest of the community saying about her? "I may not have run around like you, but that's only because I never felt a need to. I knew I wanted to join the church and looked forward to a life as a farmer's *Fraa*."

Annie's frown showed true remorse. "I'm sorry, Eva—forgive me. I just didn't want a lecture from you. I wish you were my age. Then we could sneak out together."

Sweet pastry aromas from the bakery wafted up into the apartment, a reminder that Eva had another life now, one that would never include running around with hidden phones. "I have to go to work."

"Wait." Annie put away her phone. "I overheard your prayer. Are you desiring a man you've never met?"

"Go home, Annie." Eva turned to make her way back to the door.

Annie chased after her. "You're still praying for a husband? Aren't you tired of waiting to be chosen by a man? Don't you want to go out there and do the choosing?"

"That's not how it's done. It's not the Amish way, and you know it. Now, *Heem geh*. Go home. Mamm may not say anything, but her heart will be crushed when she sees you're gone."

"But I'm not gone. I just—how do the Englisch say it?—pulled an all-nighter. That's it!" Annie smiled.

"Mamm won't know that. She might think—" Eva halted at the weight of the words she didn't want to come out of her mouth.

Annie quieted down with a sigh. "I have no plans to leave the Amish, but I'm not ready to be a Fraa. I want to wait like you did."

Eva shook her head. "Don't say that. Besides, I can name a few boys already planning on courting you next summer. With your pretty blonde hair and cornflower-blue eyes, I think you'll get to do the choosing. Don't fret about that." She forced a smile, but it turned real when her sister wrapped her arms around her and laughed.

Annie had always pushed the boundaries, not because she wanted to break the rules but to exercise some control over her life. Her gangly arms tightened around Eva. "I love you. And I love the red in your hair more than my blonde."

Eva chuckled. "We always want what we don't have. We're hopeless." She hugged her sister tightly in return. "Now go. The sun is up."

Annie ran down the outside staircase to the private entrance off the rear lot and let the door slam.

Eva hoped her aunts were too busy chatting or singing over their baking to hear it. She walked out of the apartment and shut the door behind her.

The outside door creaked open again, and Eva raised her gaze to the ceiling in frustration. "I said go home!"

"I would if I could, but I'm afraid that's not possible." The deep timbre of a man's voice froze Eva in her spot at the top of the stairs.

She took a few tentative steps closer to the staircase and saw a stranger down below. "I'm sorry. I thought you were someone else. May I help you?"

The man removed his black Amish hat to reveal silky blond hair in need of a cut, with a few strands out of place. He had no beard, and he wore jeans.

Sometimes when Amish people traveled, they dressed like the Englisch so as not to bring unwanted attention. Eva wondered if that was the case with this man.

"I'm Jacob Wittmer. I'm traveling through town, and I saw your sign in the window. I'd like to rent the apartment if it's still available."

"Traveling?" Eva's tongue stuck on the word. She had just been praying for the next tenant. Was this who she had prayed for? Eva felt her cheeks flush as she stared at the man. She hadn't imagined he would be so good-looking.

"Can I rent the apartment?" he asked, breaking through the colliding thoughts cramming her mind with questions.

I wish for this honorable man to be mine, she had written in her prayer box.

But that didn't mean *this* was the man she prayed for. It couldn't be if he wasn't Amish. Eva didn't have to pray to Gött to know she would stay Amish.

"*Ja.*" She found her voice, a squeaky one, but a voice. "It's still available."

"*Güt!*" Jacob exclaimed. "I shouldn't be in town long. A few weeks at the most. I hope that's okay with you."

"So you'll be here for Christmas?" she asked. "Won't your family miss you?" A sickening feeling filled her. Her question didn't have anything to do with respect for his family but purely selfishness on her part. She wanted to know if he was Amish.

He frowned. He must have seen through her self-seeking question.

"I apologize," Eva said quickly. "It's none of my business. Let me get my aunts. They own the building and can help you."

But before Eva could turn away, Jacob said, "I left my Amish community. I understand if you want to turn me away. I deserve it."

Honesty.

It hit Eva in an instant. This really *was* the man she prayed for. But how could it be? He wasn't Amish. He could never belong to her, and she could never belong to him. The sensible thing to do would be to send him away. Nothing but heartache would come from knowing him.

Eva opened her mouth to say so, but instead she said, "My aunts won't hold that against you. They've rented to the Englisch before."

"But I'm not Englisch. I'm banned."

"I see." Eva did see; she understood the problems his being here would cause, not only for her but for the whole community. She realized she shouldn't be speaking with him and stepped back from his view. "Let me get my aunts to show you the place."

"*Denki*—ah, I'm sorry, but I don't know your name."

She hesitated but saw no reason to withhold her identity. "Eva Stoltz."

"Miss?" Jacob asked and rushed to explain. "Your Kapp color tells me it's Miss."

"Ja, it's Miss." Eva touched her white prayer covering, reminding her of the prayers she had been saying for this man a short while ago. She prayed for Gött's guidance for a life of honor and integrity, a fresh start for *this* man, Jacob Wittmer. Her foolish heart had read more into the reasons for praying for him when he was only here for a fresh start—something Gött trusted her to help give.

Eva chided herself for once again thinking marriage was her heart's desire, even after her aunts asked her to question it. She felt free to step back into Jacob's view. She offered a welcoming smile to her visitor just as she would offer all patrons who walked through the bakery's doors.

Jacob returned one of his own, a bigger and brighter one, showing a row of even white teeth. But it was the look of admiration she caught in his vibrant blue eyes that had her stomach doing somersaults.

Eva felt her cheeks heat up, and she realized he'd misread her smile. He'd thought she was inviting him to fancy her. Eva backed out of his view again, thinking she shouldn't be alone with him if that's what he thought and regretting the fact that she didn't correct him.

Her heart pounded so loudly she could hear it in her head. She needed to get herself under control, or Rhoda and Louisa were sure to turn this handsome traveler away.

Eva took a breath and blew it out slowly, knowing she did so because deep down she wanted him to stay. But why?

Not my will but Yours, Lord.

She focused on the role she was to play in Gött's plan, the role she had always fully embraced—providing bread for a new day to everyone who walked through the bakery's door.

"Mr. Wittmer?" she called from the top of the stairs.

"I'm here," he replied.

"Come to the back door of the bakery. I'll meet you there." Eva smiled with the assurance of her place in Gött's plan for Jacob Wittmer. "Fresh bread is on the menu today, and I have some to give you."

2

Jacob Wittmer had researched Blossom Creek for nearly a year before deciding to grow his furniture business on its quaint village streets. Now, as he drove his rusty off-white pickup truck past Amish and Englisch storefronts, he knew he'd made the right decision. His Amish-crafted furniture store would fit in perfectly with the quilt and doll shop beside it, as well as the cheese shop across the street. The nearby hardware store and small grocer would bring in people from miles around, including, he hoped, many who would buy his work.

Jacob pulled up at his vacant storefront.

In doing his research, he'd found there wasn't an Amish furniture store for at least fifty miles. He envisioned a table and some chairs showcased in the big front window along the sidewalk. Maybe a desk and a coatrack behind the other display glass. But first things first: he needed to establish a good set of employees to run the place. People he could trust to make it thrive—so he could move on.

That was the plan.

Jacob would hire a few excellent furniture builders and a manager and then go on to his next venture. His goal was to open enough storefronts to make a living while he stayed out of the picture. His success in Blossom Creek would set the stage for future shops. What had started as a lonely night of brainstorming over a year ago was finally coming to fruition. He could say goodbye to begging for odd handyman jobs as he moved from town to town. He was a carpenter, but now he would be a business mogul.

Jacob shook his head at the absurdity. Never had he imagined this would be his future.

No, for twenty-three years his dream had always been to have a farm and family of his own. A life deemed worthy and Gött-fearing.

And then one night six years ago, Jacob's life took a turn. One bad decision sent him on the run.

"Mind your business, son. Gött will take care of it," Jacob's father, Moses Wittmer, had told him.

Jacob could have had his farm and family if he had heeded his father's words that night. He could have had a beautiful bride beside him to grow old with and children to raise and love. But he'd grabbed his coat and hat and walked out the door.

Now all Jacob had was a lonely life of hiding.

Mind your business. Simple words he couldn't follow six years ago, but now they were the words Jacob lived by. Minding his businesses. His future furniture businesses.

Jacob looked in his rearview mirror. The two-story white structure filling the frame glowed with a warmth he missed dearly. The sign out front read *Stoltzes' Amish Bakery: Family and Friends Welcome.*

The two sisters who owned the place had welcomed him like family. Jacob smiled. Rhoda and Louisa were funny women, happy and content. They made him feel like a family might be possible again. One glimpse at their pretty niece Eva and Jacob felt a nudge to give it a try.

His smile faded.

A family wasn't possible.

Jacob figured he had about three weeks to get his business up and running and leave town before the Stoltzes no longer considered him family or friend. He lived out of one bag, so if they learned of his past, it wouldn't take long to move out of their upstairs apartment.

He needed to be gone before his name tarnished his store. He needed to be gone before his name tarnished theirs.

Jacob parked his truck and climbed out into the three inches of new snow that had fallen the night before. He approached his new storefront and unlocked the door. A bell above chimed as he entered.

With the woodstove sitting dormant in the corner, the place felt bitterly cold. Jacob made a mental note to buy some wood later that day. He couldn't work in here like this, especially if he would have people coming in for interviews.

Jacob pictured his sideboard laden with warm coffee and pastries for his potential employees. He'd ask Eva Stoltz about a daily order. The thought of her invited another smile to invade his lips. He quickly rubbed his hand across his face to erase it along with the image of the strawberry blonde as she handed him a slice of warm bread covered in melted butter.

Maybe coming to Blossom Creek wasn't a good idea, he thought. He'd need to keep his longings for a family in check if he was going to see Eva daily. There was something about her that had stirred his old dreams this morning, and that couldn't happen again. What if she caught a glimpse of them?

Leading Eva on would be cruel. He'd make sure she knew it was best to save herself for an upstanding Amish man. She shouldn't have any trouble finding one. The men must be beating down her bakery door.

Jacob ignored the pang of jealousy that thought delivered. *I'm off to a bad start*, he chided himself as he returned to the bed of his truck and threw off the tarp draped over his handmade furniture. He reached for the pieces he could carry solo, lugging them into the store and placing them haphazardly until he could come up with a plan for a layout. On his fifth trip, he found a young Amish boy standing by his truck's tailgate.

Jacob stopped short, causing snow to fly up to his knees. "Wie geht's?" he said with a smile.

The boy appeared to be about eight years old. He had green eyes, and his hair, cut straight across his forehead, stuck out from both sides of his Amish wool hat. "I'm güt," he replied with a sweet, high-pitched voice that made Jacob like him instantly. His missing front teeth only added to his innocent charm.

"Are you here to help me carry some furniture?" Jacob walked closer to the truck.

"Are you Aunt Rhoda's and Aunt Louisa's new tenant?"

So the boy is related to the Amish bakers. That explains the charm. Jacob replied, "I sure am."

The boy gave a single nod. "Then I can help. What do you need me to do?" His little body didn't look like it could bear much weight—definitely not any of the big pieces of furniture.

Jacob searched the truck bed for something small as he said, "Your family has been most welcoming to me. And they bake delicious bread."

"Eva makes the bread, but I like her apple fry pies best. She makes them for me at home all the time."

Jacob detached a table's legs. "Is Eva your sister?" The question escaped before Jacob thought it through. What if the boy told Eva he'd asked about her? She might read more into it than she should. Jacob couldn't afford to make any more slips like this.

"Ja, she's nice but not as fun as Annie. She's my other sister."

Problem averted. Jacob was thankful for innocent minds. "Your timing is great. I was just thinking I would need an extra pair of hands to get this furniture inside, and now here you are to help. Here, take the legs of this table." He passed over two of the wooden table legs. "You can come back for the other two. Don't rush. Rushing only causes mistakes to happen."

The legs hung between them when the boy didn't make a move to accept the pieces.

"Is there a problem?" Jacob asked.

The young boy squinted up, then down the length of Jacob, then back up. "Are you Amish?"

Innocent also meant inquisitive . . . and oblivious to social proprieties. How he wished he could go back to a time when he, too, was ignorant of proper decorum.

Jacob wanted to say yes as images of Sweet Haven, Indiana, flashed in his mind. It had been six years since he could honestly say he was Amish. Not a day went by that he didn't think of his community and long to still be a part of it. He meant what he'd told Eva. If he could go home, he would. It was just not possible, not anymore.

But Jacob couldn't tell this child the truth. It wouldn't be appropriate.

"Do I look Amish?" He delayed his reply with a question as he placed the legs in the boy's waiting arms. He grabbed the tabletop from the truck and headed back to the store, hoping the conversation would naturally steer in another direction.

"Ja. But you wear jeans and I've never seen you around here before. What's your name?" The boy kicked up snow as he tried to keep up with Jacob.

They reached the door, and Jacob opened it. This was an answer he could give with no guilt. "Jacob Wittmer. This is my first day in Blossom Creek. What's your name?"

"David."

"Well, David, is there anything I should know about the place?"

"Sure! I could tell you lots. What do you want to know?"

Jacob peered down the street. Buggies sloshed by in the snow, and their horses' hooves barely made a sound. A car drove by them and splashed up the slush in a spray. "Hmm, let me think." The question of whether Eva Stoltz was courting anyone came to mind, but that would definitely get back to her. "How about you tell me where the best place to sled is?" That should be safe to ask.

The boy's face lit up with a smile, revealing the gap where his two front teeth used to be. "That's easy! Freshwater Pond down by the schoolhouse. You come flying down the hill and hit the frozen pond just right and *zoom*! You're flying so fast you can barely breathe."

"That sounds right up my alley. I'll have to give it a try while I am here. I haven't been sledding in years. Back home we had a hill that only a few brave boys ever tried. It was so steep and narrow that if you didn't turn at a certain point, you would have a mouthful of pine needles."

David giggled. "Yuck. Did you ever eat the needles?"

"Many times, if I remember correctly. My cousin never did, though, and he always reminded me of that."

"Really rubbed it in, did he?"

Jacob nodded. He hadn't thought of his sled rides in years, and David's excited face made him wonder if he dared add a sledding adventure to his list of things to do while he was in Blossom Creek. *Why not?* he thought, and then he said, "Do you think the pond is fully frozen yet? I'd love to try your hill to see if I've still got what it takes."

"Oh, it's frozen, all right. I've been out every day since—" Suddenly the boy's smile faded. He looked back at Jacob's pickup with a quizzical expression. "You have a truck. You can't be Amish."

So much for changing the subject. Jacob sighed but not because the boy was too smart to fool. For a few moments, it had felt like he belonged to a community again, to the point that he had actually entertained the notion of joining the kids for a few rides on the local sledding hill. He would be wise to remember that his course in life was set, and it didn't include communing with the Amish, not even for a toboggan ride.

Another memory of Sweet Haven flashed in his mind, but this image was the one in which the smiling faces of the people he loved turned sour and disapproving toward him. One face even turned smug.

"David," a woman's voice scolded from the corner of the building across the street. "You shouldn't be here."

Jacob half expected to see someone from his past doing the admonishing. His shame never had to travel far to surface. It was always hanging at the back of his mind, ready to remind him of his place.

"I'm sorry. I should know better," Jacob said without glancing up at the approaching woman. "I'll keep my distance from now on." He turned to face her and saw it was Eva Stoltz.

She crossed the street toward them, her black cloak swallowing her tiny frame, so much like her young brother's. She stepped up on the curb, the bottom of her maroon dress sprinkled with flour.

Jacob noticed she carried a basket inside her cloak. A white cloth covered whatever was inside. Had she brought him food? His stomach rumbled involuntarily.

"Nonsense, Mr. Wittmer. I meant that David should not be here bothering you. He comes to help at the bakery on Saturdays and after school. I went looking for him when I saw the sky." Eva looked up at the clouds closing in. "More snow, I'd say."

Without taking his eyes off her, Jacob said, "Looks like it to me." He swallowed hard. "David's fine unless you need him. In fact, he's helping me move some of these pieces in before the snow starts."

A cute little smirk curved Eva's lips. "Helping? Are you sure he's not talking your ear off and keeping you from your work? At the bakery, he's usually more of a handful than a help."

"I help!" David protested.

Eva patted her brother's head. "Yes, you do. I'm only kidding, but you should ask Mr. Wittmer if he needs help before volunteering yourself."

Even with the sun behind the thick clouds, Jacob could see the blonde hair threaded through Eva's red strands. The color was unique and mesmerizing.

She really was stunning, with a sweet-natured smile that put him at ease. Jacob found himself staring a little too long. He shook himself to refocus. Admiring Eva was only appropriate for her future husband to do. Jacob could never be a suitor for an Amish woman, and he needed to remember that.

"I'm sorry, Jacob," David said, looking up at him, his small face in a little pinch. "She doesn't understand. I'm just too little to put all the pans away. I'm going to stay here and help you carry table legs, okay?"

"David, it's Mr. Wittmer to you," Eva reprimanded.

"No, please, both of you call me Jacob. It's fine," Jacob assured her.

"All right, Jacob. Is David staying here *güt* with you?" Eva asked.

"Of course," he replied. "Extra hands are always welcome. It was the way of things in Sweet Haven."

"Sweet Haven, Indiana?" she asked, stepping closer. A spattering of light freckles covered the bridge of her nose. "We have friends in Sweet Haven. Do you know the—?"

"No," Jacob said, cutting her off. "I don't."

Eva's reddish-blonde brows furrowed. She opened her mouth as if to speak, but no words came out.

Jacob reached for the door and swung it wide. It would be best if all hopes were dashed right now. He wouldn't apologize for his rudeness, even though it pained him not to.

"David," Eva said quietly, "perhaps you should return with me. Aunt Rhoda and Aunt Louisa really need our help."

"But Jacob and I are going sledding." David followed Jacob inside. "Tell her, Jacob."

Before he could reply, Eva said, "I'm sure Jacob has to unpack today and can't take you sledding."

"I can speak for myself." Jacob spoke too quickly. As soon as the words spilled from his lips, he knew he'd taken this impoliteness too far, however prudent. Eva shouldn't be talking to him.

It's for the best, Eva Stoltz. Trust me.

"I'm sorry," she said, blushing deeply. "I just didn't want David to bother you. I figured you'd want time to get situated."

Nausea rolled through his stomach. Never had he treated anyone in such a rude manner. Women were to be treasured and respected. It was something he had learned the hard way six years ago and vowed to do from then on.

It was how he most wanted to treat Eva, but for her own good, he didn't dare.

Jacob turned away and put the table on its side. David approached with the two legs he had been carrying and helped attach them in place. He ran out the front door, sending the chimes into a song and leaving Jacob and Eva alone.

The cold room suddenly felt colder. Slowly Jacob turned to Eva, but he couldn't bring himself to meet her eyes. An apology for his behavior sat on his tongue.

"I brought you lunch," she said, breaking the silence. "I hope you like chicken. There's also some fruit and an apple spice fry pie."

Jacob dared a look at her—and nearly wept at her crestfallen expression. He'd hurt her.

The bells chimed again. "Jacob, I can't find one of the legs," David announced at the door. Frigid air rushed in behind him.

"Close the door. It's cold enough in here as it is," Eva instructed her brother.

"Keep looking. It's in there," Jacob said with his gaze still on Eva.

The boy ran back out, sealing them inside again.

Eva placed the basket down on one of Jacob's handcrafted benches and made her way to the exit. "I'll send David back with some wood to help you warm the place. We can spare some."

"No," Jacob said.

"No?" Eva turned, with a frown on her face.

Jacob managed a sad laugh. "There's no reason to be kind. That is something earned and deserved. I can get my own wood."

Eva's head tilted as she studied him openly. "Maybe you have been gone too long from your Amish community to remember, but helping others is our way, whether you think you deserve it or not."

Jacob didn't fight her on the wood, but he made his way to the basket. "This, too, is your Amish way? Or did you hope for something else from me?"

The question hung heavy in the air. He waited for her pained expression again and expected a tongue-lashing for so boldly accusing her of expecting him to ask her to go courting.

Instead Eva Stoltz stood tall and lifted her chin. "Gött sent you here for a reason. I am only doing his will." She approached the door to let David in, the missing leg now in his arms. "Enjoy your lunch." Then, turning back before she let the door close behind her, she said, "And Jacob, I changed my mind. I think you should go sledding. In fact, I think you *need* to go sledding."

Eva's buggy creaked as the horse plodded through the deep snow. It seemed to take all Keepsake's strength to pull through the powder, while more snowflakes fell on and around her. Her black mane glistened with ice crystals, and the snow covered her back so completely that it masked her bright reddish tones. Eva's Daed had handpicked Keepsake for his daughter at the auction based on the red tones alone. He'd said it was like she was part of the Stoltz family from birth, and because Eva took after his side of the family with her strawberry blonde hair, the horse was meant to be hers. Besides, Eva needed a good, strong horse to get her to work and back home to the farm every day, no matter the weather.

The sky darkened as the day neared sunset, but with the snow, Eva didn't see any evidence of the sun. It would be night soon, and Keepsake would need to work even harder. Eva wanted to find David and start back to the farm right away. The sound of children's squeals echoing through the hills told her they were close by.

The end of the road neared. She passed the one-room schoolhouse she had once attended, now closed for the weekend. A few hundred feet farther, she clucked at Keepsake to bring the buggy to a halt. Setting the brake, Eva climbed down into the deep snow. She pulled her cloak tight against the biting wind, which seemed even colder now that the sun had fallen behind the sledding hill.

Eva trudged through the snow until she reached the top of the first incline, where she spotted David and some other boys from town. But there was one sled rider taller than the rest.

Jacob Wittmer towered over the boys with his hands on his hips, laughing with just as much glee as the young ones. Eli Yoder fell, and Eva picked up her skirt to rush to his side. The boy had a twisted leg that had never grown correctly, and he needed a little more attention than the other children his age. But before she had even taken a step, Jacob lifted the boy and plopped him on the sled. Eli laughed louder than she'd ever heard him. Jacob gave him a push, and Eli slid down the hill, heading toward the frozen pond with sheer excitement.

The boys cheered exuberantly. Jacob yelled encouraging words at Eli to lean in and push on across the ice.

It was a tough task—Eva wasn't sure many of the other boys could do it, never mind Eli with his weakness. Without realizing her lips were moving, she found herself shouting along with the group, her hands clapping in their woolen mittens. When Eli touched the snow on the other side of the pond, Eva ran down the hill and across the ice along with everyone else.

"Eli! That was wonderful!" Eva reached for the small boy as he tried to pull himself out of the sled, but someone grabbed her arm.

A look of confusion crossed Eva's face as she discovered Jacob Wittmer's hand on her arm.

"Let him do it," Jacob said.

Eva shrugged her arm away, ready to give Jacob a piece of her mind for touching her so liberally, but one look at Eli standing up on his own and picking up his sled to carry back over the frozen pond made Eva realize what Jacob meant.

She had been about to assist Eli instead of waiting and letting the boy get out of the sled on his own. Eva questioned how many other times she'd moved in to help Eli without giving him a chance to handle the situation on his own or at least to try. She chided herself as she wondered if anyone had ever given Eli the opportunity to show them all what he could do.

Jacob turned away to gather the group and go back up the hill. "Well, boys, I'd say you squeezed in as much sledding as you could today. The snow is falling heavily now, and your families are going to be looking for you to come home for dinner. You best be getting on home."

"Can we sled again tomorrow after church?" Eli asked Jacob, adoration in his small dark eyes.

Jacob laid a hand on the boy's shoulder and said, "Let's wait and see what your Mamm and Daed say."

"Will you come to church with us tomorrow?" David asked as they plowed through the snow. "We're hosting."

When Jacob didn't reply, David asked again.

Eva shushed her brother, scolding him for pestering Jacob. But she did say, "Of course you are welcome to worship with our Amish community."

"I think I'm going to pass. Not really my thing. Not since I left home."

His shortness silenced the jovial group, but Eva recognized misery in his words. The pain of excommunication was felt by all the Amish. No bishop ever wanted to issue the ban, because everyone suffered. By rights, she should accept Jacob's decision to stay away, but seeing him laughing with the boys and helping Eli reinforced her belief that Gött was calling him home.

"Boys, what do you say to Jacob for taking you sledding?"

"Denki!" they all shouted, then ran up the hill, continuing their last few minutes of fun.

Eva and Jacob were left behind and walked side by side up the hill. Their time together would end when they crested the top, and somehow their steps automatically slowed.

"Did you enjoy your day of sledding?" she asked, tilting her head to see him beyond the edge of her bonnet.

Jacob's smile was back, but he didn't look at her. Instead he glanced off into the trees as though he were envisioning another time and place. "Believe it or not, I did. It felt—oh, I don't know what the word is. *Great*, maybe? No, that's not it." He shrugged. "I've never been good with words. Made my Daed disappointed in me whenever grades came home from school."

"How about *reminiscent*? Does that explain it?" Eva walked on until she realized Jacob had stopped.

Glancing downhill, she met Jacob's stunned expression staring up at her. "How did you know?" He stood with one leg bent for balance on the incline as he searched her face for the answer.

"I watched you when I arrived, or I should say, I heard you. When was the last time you laughed like that?"

He shrugged again. "Six years ago, I suppose. I left home when I was twenty-three."

"I didn't ask you when you left. I asked when you last laughed like that. Something tells me it was long before you left home."

His face fell, along with his gaze. The snow on the ground became his focus, then the top of the hill as his feet began to move again. As he passed her, he said, "I'm not worth your time, so please don't try to save me."

Eva let him go but started up the hill behind him. Eli and the other boys were already gone.

Only David sat in the buggy, waiting. He called out, "Will I see you tomorrow, Jacob?"

A forced, tight smile appeared on Jacob's lips. "I'll be at the shop."

"You're working on Sunday?" David's eyes widened in disbelief.

"I'm pretty pressed for time. I have about three weeks to get the business up and running."

"I'll help," David announced matter-of-factly. "We can go right after church."

"No, David. I'm sure your community would not want me at their church meeting."

Pouting, David retorted, "You have to come. Pleeease? Eva made all the bread. You told me you liked her bread, remember?"

"Ja, kid, I remember." Jacob glanced Eva's way, a flush creeping up from his scarf.

Oblivious to Jacob's embarrassment, David continued, "Tell him, Eva! Tell him that he'd be welcome."

Eva climbed up into her seat and grabbed the reins. "You heard him—you would be welcome. We live on Cranbrook Road. The service starts at ten."

Jacob stepped over to the buggy and offered a sad smile to David, but to Eva he said under his breath, "I'm not a *güt* Amish man. Don't make me out to be something I'm not. You'll regret it." He left her there to consider his warning.

After a few moments, she lifted a prayer to Gött for endurance. She then hit the brake and clucked at Keepsake to take them home, her mind still warring within her.

Eva couldn't be wrong about Jacob. She believed him to be the honorable man she had prayed for. Jacob Wittmer was the traveler Gött had sent. But when she prayed, Eva hadn't known just how lost this traveler was.

3

Sunday morning dawned bright and sunny with the previous day's pristine white snow glistening in the trees and over the hills. Jacob sat in his truck questioning his worthiness for what he was about to do. His soul didn't feel white as snow on a normal day, never mind on a holy day—and yet he opened his driver's door and faced the Stoltzes' family farm. The buggies lined up told him he was in the right place for the Amish community's Sunday church meeting. But being in the right place didn't mean it was right for him to be here.

He'd parked his vehicle down the road, away from the host family's home. He knew enough that no motor vehicles should ever be parked with the buggies on Sunday morning. He didn't need to bring more attention to himself.

Still, he wondered, *why am I here?*

He asked himself the question, but an image of a certain strawberry blonde with pink cheeks came to mind. Last evening's temperature wasn't the only thing that had caused her flushed complexion. Jacob knew he had alarmed her when he'd told her he wasn't the good Amish man she thought him to be.

She had insisted that he come to church at her farm. The fact that he was arriving past the time the men entered should prove his point to her.

Jacob pushed on toward the barn. Smoke billowed from the white structure's chimneys, inviting this traveler to its place of refuge. Jacob passed by a row of massive gray Percherons tossing their shaggy heads his way and jingling the bells on their reins. Their snorts sent dual puffs of white mist into the cold December air. As chilly as the morning was, Jacob stalled by the draft horses to deliberate this move.

What if someone knew his name? Eva had alluded to having friends in Sweet Haven. There were most likely others who did too. What if his name triggered memories of the events of that night six years ago in someone's mind? Jacob thought about giving a false last name, but the Stoltzes already knew the truth, and lying had never served him well—hence his living on the run. If he had told the truth in the first place, he might never have had to leave. If he had told the truth, maybe it would have been Peter who left instead.

Not a chance. No one would have believed him over Peter. They never did. Leaving was Jacob's only choice.

And rejoining an Amish community could never be. *So why try?*

Jacob made his decision and pivoted sharply to return to his truck. Turning, he caught sight of the women entering the side entrance of the barn. The men had already entered through their section, and the women were next.

A splash of reddish-blonde hair halted his steps. Eva's hair shone brightly against her white Kapp. Her green eyes burned through him. She watched him with such intent that he could practically read her mind. He could see she thought he was a worthy man. He should tell her the truth to prove to her the error of her ways.

Eva pointed toward the barn door the men went through.

Jacob offered a slight nod of apology and headed toward his truck. He picked up his pace, knowing she continued to watch him. He forced himself not to break into a full sprint. She'd already seen him turn tail. She didn't have to see him run too.

What does it matter what Eva Stoltz thinks of me, anyway?

Jacob didn't know the answer to that, but he knew it did matter. In some strange way Eva had the power to infiltrate his life of hiding. Coming to Blossom Creek had been a bad idea.

Jacob neared his truck. He planned to get in and get out of town. He'd research another place to build his business. Ohio was a big state. On second thought, maybe another state, one that didn't have Eva Stoltz in it, would be best.

Jacob skidded on a patch of ice and grabbed on to his truck's side mirror to steady himself. A look over the hood showed Eva still standing in her spot, now alone. All the other women and girls were gone.

The wind whipped her black cloak against her green skirt and white apron. Slowly she removed her right hand from its warmth behind the wool fabric and extended it to him.

Komm.

He could practically hear the invitation in her sweet voice. The goodness of it tormented him. She didn't know what she was asking for.

Scandal, embarrassment, *trouble.*

Her hand stayed put, and Jacob took a step toward her.

The trip back to the barn seemed like an eternity, but with Eva as his focal point, the rest of the world around him fell away. The buggies and horses blurred, and so did his past. If only it were that easy.

"You don't know what you're inviting," he said in a low voice as he neared her. "I should leave here right now and never come back."

Eva nodded. "I would pray for you."

"No, Eva. You need to forget you ever met me. And never pray for me."

"Too late. I already have." Her eyes glimmered bright. "Gött put you in my heart the morning you arrived."

Jacob should have scoffed, but hearing how she had lifted him to Gött flooded him with a feeling that till now had always eluded him.

All he could do was take another step closer to this woman who made him feel . . . safe.

Her hand dropped back to her side, but she left it out of her cloak. Her delicate skin chafed under the frigid wind.

"You should go inside," he told her. "It's too cold."

"I'll go in when the last man has entered the building."

Jacob shook his head, removing his black-brimmed hat to hold at his front. "I'm not that man, Eva. You need to know that. I'm not that man you prayed for."

"Gött will decide who you are, Jacob Wittmer. And I will follow His will."

The barn door behind her creaked open. Rhoda Stoltz peeked her head out with a warning look their way. "Bishop will be starting soon."

Eva looked back at him. "Well? What do you say?"

"I say you'll regret this." Jacob took a deep breath and let it go. "Gött's will be done."

Eva's huge smile pulled his gaze to her full lips. The woman was stunning, possessing a striking beauty that grew out of wisdom.

Jacob turned away from her to approach the door the men entered through. He could only pray that she was indeed making a wise choice by inviting him into her community.

From her place at the back of the women's side of the barn, Eva barely felt the heat from the woodstoves up front, and yet she burned with nervousness. Aunt Rhoda's pinched lips beside her didn't help. Eva had chosen a seat in the last row of benches to avoid inquiring eyes when she entered the barn late, but she should have known her aunts would see through her actions. Doubts filtered through her mind about why she had invited Jacob here today. With her fingers clasping and unclasping in her lap, she slowly lifted her chin a bit to see through the wide doorway into the men's side of the barn.

Bishop Roy Swartzentruber spoke from a portal that separated the two rooms. With all her fidgeting and worries about Jacob being somewhere on the men's side, she honestly hadn't heard a word of his sermon so far.

Eva squinted beyond Bishop and peered between Eli Yoder and his father's head. She could see Jacob's hair, and when he tilted his head, half of his face came into view.

Eva's fingers stopped the moment she saw him. The tightness in her chest released as she sighed deeply. Whether she had made the right choice in inviting him here remained to be seen, but she couldn't argue with what his presence offered her—a peace she hadn't felt in a long time. Since long before Daniel's letter, if she was being honest. Annie's harsh words had been lingering at the back of Eva's mind. *You're just jealous because you gave up your Rumspringa to make Daniel King think you were marriage-worthy. You wasted years waiting for him.*

And during those years, Eva had never been able to truly relax, always worrying that she wasn't good enough for Daniel. And in the end, she hadn't been.

Maybe that was why she could relax with Jacob. She already knew she wasn't marriage-worthy, so she could focus on helping him instead. It didn't help that he was so handsome, though.

Eva smiled across the ladies' heads, all topped with their prayer coverings. Jacob was listening intently to Bishop Roy, oblivious to her peeking at him. Eva especially liked the way his hair curled at the nape of his neck. Her fingers itched to loop themselves through the curls to feel their silkiness. She flushed at the direction of her thoughts and lowered her face before someone noticed.

Aunt Rhoda jabbed her with her elbow.

So much for going unnoticed. But when Eva faced Rhoda, the smirk on her aunt's lips eased her guilt. Not enough to attempt another glance Jacob's way, however.

Eva forced herself to listen to Bishop Roy's deep voice.

"Children of Gött are called to . . ."

Another deep voice resurfaced in her mind. She recalled Jacob's laugh on the hill the day before. Soon her mind took flight on another departure from the service. From beneath her lashes her mind flitted to an open buggy ride after church. She nearly giggled aloud at the scene her mind conjured up. With the cold, they would need heavy blankets to stay warm.

Eva closed her eyes and immersed herself in her daydream. She could hear the deep rumble of Jacob's laugh. He sounded so carefree as they raced through the hills on their buggy ride. She imagined turning to him and reaching out to touch the curls at his neck. Only when he turned to her, it was Daniel's face she saw—looking at her with revulsion.

Eva sat up straight on her bench. Her sudden movement caused Aunt Rhoda to send her a heated look, the smirk long gone.

"I'm sorry," Eva mouthed and dropped her head again, this time in shame. The need to repent overcame her, and she prayed silently for forgiveness. Gött had not sent Jacob here to court her. She needed to let her wish go.

I wish for this honorable man to be mine.

Her wish seemed trivial now, knowing how lost Jacob was. Gött hadn't brought Jacob to Blossom Creek for her to marry, no matter what she wished for or believed to be her heart's desire. *I'm acting like a schoolgirl*, she chastised herself. *The man needs community. He needs to belong.* Jacob needed to step into his identity of that man of integrity Eva had prayed for. And he needed to do this for his own reconciliation, not for any selfish desire on her part.

Bishop cleared his throat loudly, and Eva's head shot up. He now faced the women's side, but he appeared to be looking only at her.

Eva perused the room to see the women turning to look at her too. Had Bishop called her name and she'd missed it in her daydreaming?

Aunt Rhoda nudged her. "Go on. He called you up there."

Eva stood uncertainly. She brushed her white apron straight down in front of her, pulling the back of her dress down as well. Her boots clunked on the wood floor like heavy blocks, or perhaps it only seemed that way to her as she made her way past all the women with the men in the other room staring her down.

Finally she reached the bishop. "B-bishop?"

"Eva, you brought a guest today, did you not?"

"He—ja, Bishop, I did." Eva nodded and stole a glance Jacob's way before looking back at the bishop. "Jacob Wittmer is visiting from Indiana. Sweet Haven. He is staying at my aunts' bakery apartment for a few weeks while he establishes his furniture store. I hope it's *güt* that I welcomed him here."

A silence weighed her down, but Eva kept her chin up as she waited for the bishop's response. Roy Swartzentruber's word would set the stage for how everyone else in the community would treat Jacob. If his answer was no, then they would all need to obey his command and send Jacob away. As much as Eva would hate to do so, she would obey her bishop.

At twenty-one she had entered the church on her own, turning her back on the Englisch world. At the time, she had hoped Daniel would notice she was ready to be a *güt* Amish Fraa and court her, but even then he had shown signs of indifference. If only she had been honest with herself instead of having stars in her eyes and seeing what was never there.

She could only trust in Gött that she wasn't repeating her error.

"Jacob," Bishop called, turning toward him. "Komm."

Jacob stood warily.

Eva sent him a smile to try to ease his concern. Bishop was a stern but kind man. Gött had chosen well when He picked Roy Swartzentruber to oversee their community.

Without his hat, Jacob looked so young, almost like a schoolboy anticipating a punishment from his teacher. Eva hoped no punishment was coming. But why would there be? Jacob hadn't done anything wrong, had he?

His warnings to her niggled at the back of her mind as the bishop spoke, pulling her away from her worrying thoughts.

"As bishop of Blossom Creek, allow me to welcome you to our community. We are happy to meet you and have you here, especially your new business. Please join us for dinner following the service."

A sigh escaped from someone. When Bishop raised his eyebrows in her direction, she realized it must have been her.

"Denki, Bishop," Jacob said and extended a hand for the bishop to shake. "I would be most appreciative to join you, but I already have plans to visit a friend today. May I have another opportunity?"

"Of course," Bishop said. "You must join me for dinner tomorrow."

Jacob blanched and swallowed. More and more, he resembled a boy in trouble. "Tomorrow is perfect. Thank you. And thank you to the Stoltz family for renting me the apartment during my short stay. I'm more than satisfied that I have chosen the right place for my store, and I look forward to hiring some of you"—Jacob nodded to the men behind him—"to run my shop. Please come see me this week if you are interested. Not today, of course, it being the Sabbath."

Bishop's stern composure broke into a grin, and Eva wondered if he noticed Jacob's nervousness. How could anyone miss it? But why? Bishop welcomed him. Jacob should be happy.

Before she could figure it out, Eva and Jacob were dismissed back to their seats to finish the service. Soon they were all sent on their way and headed out to break bread with the members. As Eva went with her family to prepare the tables, she looked for Jacob. Not seeing him, she looked outside, in the direction of his truck.

It was gone from its parking place.

Jacob had left before anyone else could approach him. Again, she could only ask herself why. What was Jacob afraid of? Was he worried they'd find out he left his community? Or perhaps he worried they would learn the reason he left. Maybe Jacob hadn't been given a choice.

"Jacob seems like a nice young man." Mamm stepped up from behind her with Daed beside her.

Sarah and Aaron Stoltz were complete opposites in their temperaments. Eva's father tended to be more judgmental than his wife. Where her mother saw a nice young man, her father formed other conclusions.

"I'd like to meet him," Mamm continued. "Would you introduce me to your friend?"

"Um, he had to leave right away," Eva said.

"Oh, he did say he had a meeting with a friend today. Do you know if it's an Amish friend from a nearby community?"

"I'm not sure. Maybe." Eva had a feeling there was no friend at all, that Jacob had retreated to his shop to work. She didn't dare suggest to her parents that he was working on the Sabbath or that he had lied to the bishop about it.

Whatever had made Jacob leave his community wouldn't let go of him, even six years later. Whatever had happened scared him enough to lie to them today.

"Jacob is a very *güt*-looking man, but I suppose you already recognized that," Mamm said to Eva with a knowing smile.

Eva looked at her father. He wore a frown on his bearded face. She said to her mother, "He is but I just want to help him. That is all."

Daed huffed. "All I will say is be careful, Eva. You're thinking with your heart again. That can only lead to trouble."

4

Monday morning Eva entered the bakery and greeted Aunt Rhoda and Aunt Louisa, who were in the middle of a conversation. She halted in an instant when she noticed her aunts' drawn faces. "Am I interrupting something?"

Tight smiles were their response. Eva could count on one hand the times the two typically jovial women had acted this way.

"Is something wrong?" she asked, slowly untying her cloak.

Rhoda went back to kneading dough.

Louisa shook her head and said, "Not at all. I started the ovens. Why don't you make the fry pies today? I'll need you to run them over to a breakfast at the senior center. They ordered fifty, apple spice and cherry."

So, it is to be all business today.

Eva finished putting her things away and began preparations for cooking. She put on her white work apron and washed up. Gathering a basket of apples from the root cellar, she returned to the tense atmosphere.

Something was wrong, and her aunts weren't telling her what. Had they figured out that Jacob lied yesterday? They would be the two to know these things.

Eva peeled, cut, poured, and stirred, while no one said a word. After half an hour without a joke or a song that always made working there so enjoyable, Eva put the first batch of fry pies into hot oil and turned to her aunts. "Please, I know something is wrong. Why are you shutting me out? Have I done something to deserve to be punished like this?"

"*Ach! Neeh.*" Rhoda threw down her rolling pin into a cloud of flour and wiped her hands on her apron. "This doesn't concern you."

Louisa grunted. "Of course it does. You've seen the way she looks at the man. The whole community has seen the way she looks at him now."

"Man?" It *was* about Jacob.

"Jacob Wittmer," Rhoda confirmed.

"What about him? Is he gone?" Eva knew her voice's tremor gave away her fear for Jacob's whereabouts. She busied herself by checking the fry pies but glanced in the direction of the stairs.

"He's still here," Louisa said. "For now."

"For now? You're going to evict him?"

Louisa continued, "I know you don't like it, but we have no other choice. We could be in a great deal of trouble if Bishop learns we knew about what he's done."

They know Jacob lied. "Please, shouldn't we talk to him first and ask him to explain and allow him to repent? That's our way."

"It's not us he needs to repent to. It's his community in Indiana."

"Jacob did something to his community? I was hoping—I was praying there wasn't a terrible reason why he left." Eva's stomach rolled. Avoiding their eyes, she removed the fry pies from the oil and put in another batch. "Is it bad?" *Is it hopeless for Jacob's redemption?*

Louisa reached inside a drawer and pulled out an old copy of *The Budget*, an Amish newspaper. She unfolded the yellowed paper to an article titled *Young Amish Woman Dies. Jacob Wittmer Flees.*

Eva's breath caught in her chest, her heart ached, and yet she couldn't stop reading.

The article mentioned a young woman named Lily falling to her death. Jacob had been there. From there the words blurred, none of them making sense in Eva's mind. She stepped back and planted herself on the three-legged stool, her legs wobbling as much as the stool's unsteady leg. "Do they think he caused the young woman to die? Do they think he committed *der Mord*?"

"It doesn't say," Rhoda said. "But it does say Jacob has been shunned. That means we should honor—"

"How?" Eva interjected.

"Pardon? How what?" Rhoda asked.

"How did you find this? How did you know to go look for it?"

"You know we keep all the papers. We have them for years back. After services yesterday, someone mentioned recognizing his name but couldn't recollect where. They thought maybe they read about Jacob in one of the Amish papers. We came back here and searched the past issues. I'm sorry, Eva. I honestly didn't think it would be for something this horrible. But it won't be long before others find it too."

Eva jumped to her feet. "A young woman died. It doesn't say anything about Jacob causing it. It just says he was there, right?"

"Ja, I suppose so. But he's shunned. He ran. That says—"

"That says he was scared. That's all," Eva insisted. "I know he is a man of integrity and honor." She looked at the date written on the paper.

Six years ago—just as he'd said.

The paper shook in her trembling hands. "Jacob, what happened to make you afraid to stay?" Eva said softly. "It had to be something worse than the life of solitude you've chosen instead."

"How do you know this, child?" Louisa asked. "Ach, the pies!" She rescued them before they burned, and dunked another batch into the oil.

The fragrant aroma of apple spice filled the kitchen. Normally Eva would have inhaled the pleasurable scent, but right now something seemed rotten. She couldn't believe that Jacob was guilty of something so heinous as murder. There had to be more to the story.

"Gött sent Jacob here. I prayed for him—a traveler, but I hadn't realized he would be this lost," Eva admitted. "I see now that I am to continue to pray for him. Evicting him would be dire to him. Please, I beg of you, let him stay."

"A young woman is dead. They found her on a vacant farm. Why was she there? Why was Jacob there?" Louisa asked. "The paper says he called the police. He had a cell phone. What *güt* Amish man has a cell phone? There must be more to Jacob Wittmer than we know. I think he should go."

Eva gave her attention to Rhoda. What would she say? Would she side with her sister? Or would she give Eva the benefit of the doubt?

Rhoda showed her indecision with a loud sigh. She closed her eyes and rubbed her forehead with the back of her hand. "I trust your instincts, Eva. I do. But—"

"It's almost Christmas," Eva interrupted. "Jacob needs us. Gött needs us to lead Jacob back to Him. Something happened that's not written in that paper. Let's wait before sending him away. Let's pray for guidance before we make the decision."

"You're thinking with your heart," Louisa accused, just as Eva's father had said the day before. Did her Daed and aunts see something Eva couldn't see in herself? Was she incapable of making this decision because she had wished for an honorable man to be hers?

"If Jacob killed this young woman, then he is not the honorable man I prayed for," Eva said. "If he didn't kill her, then he needs an honorable person to stand by him."

A heavy silence fell over the room until a knock on the back door broke the void.

The door creaked opened. "Mmm. The smells floated up to my apartment and pulled me down here." Jacob walked into the bakery, dressed for a day of work, his hair still a bit damp. "I'll take whatever that delicious smell is."

His smile brought in the sunshine just coming up over the trees. Eva attempted to smile back at him but failed miserably.

Slowly his own smile dimmed. "Did I say something wrong? Should I come back later?" He searched the three solemn faces before him.

"No," Louisa said. She stuffed the newspaper back into the drawer and turned around to face them all. "Stay. Eva tells us you've been traveling a long time. This is your home, for however long you need it to be."

"It's official," Jacob announced. "You make the best apple spice fry pies I've ever had. And I've been to many bakeries in my travels. These are blue-ribbon all the way."

"We're not looking for a blue ribbon," Louisa called from the table where she was busy bagging loaves of bread. Her lips fought against a smile. "But it's good to know where we stand. Or I should say where Eva stands. After all, she is our pastry chef and fry pie maker. She has a skill, for sure."

Jacob took another bite of his fry pie. *So good but not as good as its maker.*

Eva took her aunt's praise with a sweet humility he found endearing. The tilt of her head may have been her way of shielding her gentle smile, but she couldn't hide the blush that crept into her cheeks. She waved off his praise and returned to her work at the stove.

"It's okay to be good at something," he said. "Gött has given us talents. I would say that you've found yours."

The front doorbell rang. A customer entered, and Eva wiped her hands on her apron and dashed off through the swinging doors to the front, saved from accepting his praise.

Jacob peered through the window and watched her take her place behind the large glass counter. The day's pastries and breads were displayed inside, and the customer had trouble making his choice. Jacob didn't blame him, but his own eyes kept returning to the woman behind the counter.

Eva glanced up and caught Jacob looking her way. He expected her to smile, but he glimpsed concern on her face instead. Something was wrong with Eva today. He'd sensed it the moment he entered the bakery, and he was sure of it now.

"Is Eva feeling well today?" he asked Rhoda and Louisa. "She doesn't seem her sure and sweet self."

The two women glanced at each other before Rhoda said, "She's received some news today that upset her, but she's stronger than you think. Stronger than we all gave her credit for."

"I'm beginning to see that." Jacob ate the last bite of his fry pie and wiped his hands on the cloth napkin Eva had handed him along with it. He continued to watch her handle the customers coming in one after the other. She met each one with a genuine smile and a warm welcome and seemed to know what each one liked the best.

"She sees people," Jacob murmured to himself. Did he dare trust her with who he really was? With what he had done?

No. Never.

Jacob tossed the napkin onto the counter and made his way to the back door.

"Weren't you going to say goodbye?" Eva suddenly appeared. She stood in the doorway, holding the swinging door wide.

He stopped with his hand on the doorknob. "I have to get to work." The excuse somehow sounded lame, even though the Amish valued a strong work ethic.

"I see. Shall I hold a fry pie for you tomorrow too?"

"I don't want to wear out my welcome."

Eva smiled. "Impossible. This is your home."

The mention of home brought on a wave of melancholy he hadn't expected to feel. As quaint as the Amish bakery was, it wasn't home. Not the dream Jacob had carried with him of a place to call home. Blossom Creek was just a port he could only pass through. Jacob had been to many places these past six years, but never had he felt the longing for home that Blossom Creek instilled in him.

But then, none of those places had Eva Stoltz.

"You're a beacon of light, Eva, to this lonely road I travel. Thank you for welcoming me."

A sad smile spread on her pretty lips. He would have liked nothing more than to kiss the sadness from them, but Jacob forced his mind to forge a new path from the direction it went. Any longer and he would give his thoughts away. He had to be sure he never gave Eva cause to believe there could be something between them. As soon as his business was up and running, he would be back on that long, lonely road.

"It is not my light you see but the Lord's," Eva said quietly.

"Maybe, but you also have a glow about you that reaches out to people and tells them they're safe with you. I knew it the first moment we met, and I see it with your customers."

The bell rang out in the store again. Another patron pulled Eva's attention away. She looked through the doorway and said, "Hello, Sheriff Murphy."

A tall, uniformed lawman stepped in. He removed his brimmed hat to expose a balding head with wisps of thinning hair. "The regular today, Miss Stoltz. An apple fry pie and a coffee."

"I'll be with you in one moment."

The lawman nodded and then noticed Jacob through the door.

He squinted in speculation and said, "Visiting Blossom Creek?"

Jacob had no time to back out of view. "Ja, for a few weeks," he replied, hoping that would be the end of the conversation. He typically steered clear of law enforcement, unsure of what his community back in Indiana might have done to track him down. He knew some would like to know his whereabouts. One man in particular.

Eva said, "Sheriff, this is Jacob Wittmer. He's renting the apartment upstairs while he opens the vacant shop down the street."

"Oh yeah? What do you sell?"

"Furniture," Jacob replied. "Amish crafted."

"You ex-Amish?" The sheriff's stern composure worried Jacob. He could probably count on the man doing a search on him, and now that Eva had given him his name, it wouldn't take him long to figure out that he was on the run and why.

"Yes, I left my community to be Englisch. Speaking of my business, I need to be on my way if I want to open up on time. *Güt* day to you all."

"Don't forget you have lunch with the bishop," Eva called as he quickly retreated.

How could I forget? Setting up a store in Blossom Creek was proving to be risky. First the sheriff was asking questions, and now he had to partake in a meal with the bishop. "I'll be there," he confirmed with false enthusiasm.

"Take a loaf of bread off the counter. The Swartzentrubers will like that."

"*Güt* idea. Denki." Jacob picked up a bagged loaf and bolted out the door before he could be called back for more questions. A teenage girl was coming in at the same time, and Jacob nearly bowled her over in his escape.

"Annie!" Eva cried and rushed over to the teenager. Jacob instantly saw why Eva was concerned. In his hasty retreat, he hadn't noticed a bruise on Annie's face. "What happened?" Eva asked as she reached for her.

"It's nothing. I fell on some ice. I came to get cleaned up before going home. I don't want Mamm to see me."

Aunt Rhoda brought a rag with some ice and told Annie to sit. The older woman shook her head with a *tsk* as she assessed Annie's face.

Rumspringa, Jacob guessed as he stepped out to leave the family to care for their own. He closed the door, knowing the adults would look the other way while the teenager ran free. He remembered his own years of running—and the fact that he had never stopped.

5

"Welcome, Jacob, to our home. This is my Fraa, Emma." Bishop Roy Swartzentruber took Jacob's coat and hung it on the peg by the family's front door. The older man had a neat, straight beard the color of snow, and Emma's soft hair matched his in the same hue.

"Thank you for honoring me with the invitation. I brought some bread. I hope you like it."

"Bread from the Stoltzes' bakery? Of course." Emma's face lit up as she took it. "It will go well with our soup. Denki."

Emma led Jacob, with the bishop behind him, down a hall into the kitchen at the back of the old farmhouse. She laid the table with a simple meal of vegetable beef soup, salad, and the bread from the bakery. Jacob waited for Bishop Swartzentruber to sit at the head of the table, followed by Emma across from him, before sitting between them.

"It's just the two of us now," Bishop Roy began. "The children are all grown and married. My son has built himself a home for his family on the property, so this is now the *Grossdaadi Haus*." The man smiled broadly.

The bishop's expression stumped Jacob. He didn't think he'd ever seen Bishop Güngerich back in Sweet Haven smile like that. If he had, maybe Jacob could have gone to him when the trouble started. Then again, the trouble had started because of his son, so probably not, no matter how much the bishop smiled.

"Can you tell us about your family, Jacob?"

Jacob opened his mouth to speak, but the words tripped over

each other. The next second he could feel his leg shaking under the table. He put a hand on his thigh to control it and took a deep breath before starting again. "My family, let's see. My Mamm and Daed are Moses and Ruthie Wittmer. I'm an only child. No siblings."

"An only child?" Bishop's eyebrows arched to the ceiling.

"It wasn't by choice. My Mamm would have loved to have more, but it wasn't Gött's will."

"It must have been nice to have your parents' undivided attention growing up. Was it your Daed who taught you your woodworking skill?"

"Some. He's a farmer, and with only one son, he didn't have much time for teaching me how to work with wood. He would grow angry with me when he would find me whittling in the barn."

"I see," the bishop said, glancing at his wife.

Jacob knew that neither of them could really understand the wedge between him and his father. The bishop had a loving family still on the property. They were obviously a tight-knit group.

"And how does your Daed feel about you opening furniture businesses in Amish communities?"

Jacob didn't want to lie to this man again. Making up the story of meeting with a friend the day before to get out of having dinner with him hadn't worked in the end, as here he was having lunch instead. But what could he say? That his Daed had no idea where his son was? That they hadn't seen each other in six years?

"I'm sure it bothers him," Jacob replied with the only truth he could offer. "The things I did growing up tended to bother him a lot."

The bishop and Emma shared a concerned look that Jacob thought for sure would turn into a lecture on the ramifications of speaking of his father in a negative manner.

Surprisingly, though, the next thing spoken was from Emma when she said, "*Mann*, shall we pray?"

Bishop Roy agreed, and they all bowed their heads and asked Gött to bless their food. When they lifted their heads, Bishop requested that Jacob pass him the bread. Jacob passed the cutting block to the bishop, and as the man took a piece of bread, he said pointedly, "Eva is a wonderful baker."

"Yes, she is. I had the opportunity to see her at work today." Jacob offered the block to Emma for her piece before taking his own. "I can't understand why she isn't married. Surely the men in your community see how wonderful she is." He buttered his bread and took a bite. *Mmm, delicious.*

"So she hasn't told you, then," Bishop said.

Jacob paused in his chewing, then swallowed the piece whole before saying, "I'm not sure I know what you're speaking of."

"Well, as you said, she is a wonderful person and a fantastic cook. There have been suitors interested in courting her, but Eva had her heart set on someone in particular. I believe the other men respected her choice and stepped back."

"So then why isn't she married?"

"Her suitor decided to marry another. He left a couple of weeks ago for someone else in another community. It was difficult for Eva, especially after seeing something in him she thought was worth waiting for. And she waited a long time."

Jacob's stomach turned at the thought of eating another bite. "What did she see in him?"

"That would be a question for her. I can only surmise, knowing Eva's kind heart, that she saw goodness in him. She wouldn't settle for anything less. She always encourages people to be the best they can be."

Jacob stirred his soup in a slow circle. "Such as honorable," he said, thinking about what she'd said she saw in him.

"Ja." The bishop took a sip of his soup.

Jacob realized he was still stirring his soup. He put the spoon down. "Why are you telling me this?"

The bishop followed Jacob's lead and put his own spoon down. Looking squarely into his eyes, Bishop asked, "Jacob, do you have plans to walk out with Eva?"

Again Jacob floundered for words, but Bishop's penetrating stare motivated him to find them without delay. "I think it would be best if I moved on without starting something. Especially if she's already been hurt."

Bishop nodded and took a bite of Eva's bread. "Then I think it would be best if you move on as quickly as possible."

Jacob half-heartedly picked up a hammer and climbed the ladder to hang a sign in his shop. He'd just returned from lunch with Bishop Roy and his wife. He couldn't say he was still hungry, because he had struggled to finish his meal. His unsettled stomach had nothing to do with the company and everything to do with doing the right thing.

The right thing, of course, was to leave Blossom Creek—when he didn't really want to.

Jacob liked the accepting people of this community. He liked their smiling bishop. He liked his village shop. The idea of leaving it all behind in a few weeks bothered him. But nothing bothered him as much as the thought of leaving Eva.

That was the real struggle.

The meaning was clear; Jacob didn't need it spelled out for him. He knew it every time he looked into Eva's eyes. She saw him as some charity case. He wondered if she took in stray animals too. But she also looked at him as something more. Something he couldn't give her.

Just like the man she had waited for couldn't.

She'd been hurt once by someone. Jacob couldn't be the one to do it again.

The bell to the shop jingled, pulling Jacob out of his thoughts. He stepped down from the ladder as a young Amish man in his early twenties stepped inside and stomped his snow boots on the rug.

"Merry Christmas," the man said.

Jacob put down his hammer to welcome the visitor. "We're not open yet, but if there's something I can help you with, I will try."

"I'm Luke Beiler. I was in church yesterday when you mentioned you needed carpenters for your store." He removed his hat. "I would like to apply."

"I see." It looked like Jacob's dilemma of getting out of town sooner rather than later was about to be solved for him.

Unless he turned the young man away. Jacob rationalized that Luke was far too young to trust with his business, but then Jacob had been about the same age when he left Sweet Haven.

"Do you have carpentry experience?"

"Ja sir. My Daed and I have a woodshop in the barn. We're always building something. Chairs, benches, toys—you name it, I can build it." A blush crept up his neck. "I was married a few weeks ago." He rubbed his chin, showing the slight growth coming in. "So I've moved out of my home now."

"Congratulations. Now you're looking for a job to support your wife."

"We're living with her parents for now but—"

"You'd like to find your own place," Jacob finished for him.

Luke offered a sheepish grin, but Jacob couldn't fault the young man. Not when Luke had the life Jacob envied. "I've been saving for a while, but with winter, work's pretty slow."

"Not for furniture. People are always in need around the calendar. I hope to keep you busy. Are you able to take orders and ship? I'm thinking that much of my business will be online orders from non-Amish people looking for finely crafted furniture. Are you all right with that?"

Luke's face fell. "I will have to ask Bishop."

"I've just come from having lunch with him. We discussed it. I also explained that my workers will not have to take the orders directly from technological sources but rather through a manager—maybe Englisch or Mennonite—who has access to computers and phones. I understand that you can't use technology."

"Then, yes, I can take orders and ship. I'd love to show you what I can do."

"Great. Let's get started." Jacob led the way to a room at the back of the store where he'd set up a woodworking shop with nonelectric hand tools arranged in an orderly fashion on shelves and in cabinets. He waved a hand at the assortment and said, "Surprise me."

In a flurry of excitement, Luke jumped right in, taking down the tools he needed to begin. Wood of various cuts and lengths was piled in the storage shed attached to the back of the store. He retrieved what he wanted and got to work.

It didn't take Jacob long to see that the young man was right at home and a good craftsman. He watched appreciatively as Luke took exceptional care in his measuring and cutting. "Measure twice. Cut once," he said to Jacob over his shoulder, repeating the familiar adage aloud before he set the saw to cut.

The front door's bell jingled. Jacob left Luke to attend to the visitor, but as soon as he saw Eva standing by the door, he halted in his tracks, remembering what the bishop had shared about her broken engagement.

Who was he, Eva? Does your heart still hurt? I would never hurt you—if I was free to love you.

"Hello, Eva," was all that Jacob could manage.

She pulled on the strings of her satchel, wrapping them around her fingers in a nervous gesture. "Hello. I was passing by after making my deliveries. I have to talk to you about something. It's been on my mind all day, but I see you're not alone. I can come back."

"No." Whatever weighed Eva down was enough to pale her skin and speed up her breathing. She looked frightened. But of what? Not him, he hoped. "I'm free now. Do you want to sit down?"

Eva bit her lower lip. The sawing continued without a break, and she looked over to the back room where Luke was visible through the open door. "My cousin is working for you?"

Jacob glanced behind him. "Luke is your cousin?" He turned back to find tears sparkling in Eva's eyes. Everything else was forgotten. The only thing that mattered to Jacob was Eva and taking away whatever was bothering her.

Jacob stepped closer to her, reaching for her hand with all his attention on her. "No, Eva, don't cry. Tell me how to fix it." *It kills me to see you hurting. Please, don't let it be because of me.*

Eva shook her head and looked at his hand wrapped around hers. "So gentle. These are not hands that could hurt anyone, are they, Jacob?"

"Do you think I hurt someone?" His heart lurched. *What if she did?*

Eva raised her chin, and the tears stopped. A look of defiance filled her eyes now. "No I do not. You are a good and honorable man. I believe that with all my heart. I don't care what they say."

"Who says?" *She knows . . . something. But it's not the whole story.*

"My aunts. They're concerned about me spending time with you, but they needn't be. Here you are giving work to my family, my cousin who needs a job so he can provide for his wife. This is who you are. A caring man who wants to help this community thrive."

Jacob released her hand, though it cost him. He had to end this now. "Your aunts are right to be concerned about you spending time with me. Giving Luke a job is nothing more than a professional decision to get my business up and running quickly. It's purely selfish, for my own gain. I just want to get out of town quickly."

Shock cast a shadow over her beautiful face. Her full round lips drew in a sharp breath.

Jacob knew he had insulted her. His rejection of her words communicated that he considered her unintelligent. He might as well have called her stupid outright. The idea came to his mind to say it. It might be just what was needed to make her stay away for good.

But the words wouldn't form. He had to draw a line even he couldn't cross.

"I should return to the bakery." She fumbled for the doorknob.

"Here, let me." Jacob reached behind her and came within an inch of her face. They froze at the proximity between them, realizing the charge of electricity could have powered the saw Luke hand-cranked in the back of the store.

Jacob's eyes closed of their own accord. He couldn't move away if he wanted to, and truth be known, he wanted nothing more than to take Eva in his arms and never let her go. He opened his eyes to see her staring at him. Still, he couldn't release her.

"I don't believe you, Jacob," Eva whispered. "Just so you know. I don't believe you are as selfish as you claim."

"How can you be so sure?" He hoped his eyes held the same severity as hers. But he nearly closed them again to stop her from seeing into his soul.

"Because if you were a selfish man, you would have kissed me just now—and you didn't. That's all I need to know." With that she turned away, opened the door, and stepped out into the dreary afternoon.

The bell jingled and the door closed on a whoosh of cold air, but Jacob stood frozen in place. It wasn't until his hands ached from clenching them together so tightly that he realized how much effort he'd expended to keep from grabbing Eva and kissing her tempting lips.

He would never cross a line like that, and now Eva knew it. Making her think less of him had just gotten harder.

6

A full week passed without a glimpse of Jacob. Eva immersed herself in the busy Christmas season with extra orders of holiday pies and cookies. A flurry of cheerful visits from patrons and friends gave the bakery a festive atmosphere. Gött was at the center of the holiday. There were no decorations or even a Nativity scene in the Amish business, for displaying a graven image was not allowed. The only embellishments were Christmas cards adorning the doorways and candles in the windows glowing brightly as a welcome to the Christ Child—and to wandering travelers.

One in particular.

Eva stood by the window watching fresh snowflakes float down over the Monday-morning streets. She lit the last single candle and placed it on the sill. It glowed warm and bright against the backdrop of the winter wonderland outside.

She looked for evidence of Jacob's truck tires in the snow. She hadn't seen him since the day at his shop. Each morning Eva saved an apple spice fry pie for him, but when he didn't show up on the first day, she knew he was putting some distance between them. She didn't expect anything less from him. It was the honorable thing to do.

Jacob planned to leave after his shop was established and running. He also had a past he kept hidden. Eva wished she could have told him what her aunts had learned of the situation. Holding on to guilt and shame ate away at a person. Jacob was on the run from whatever happened six years ago. But what would she say if he did confide in her? She could offer no resolution to his past. All she could offer him was an apple spice fry pie.

And so, she did.

Each morning Eva left a warm fry pie in a small box with a red bow on his doorstep. She would then watch him walk across the street to his store, knowing he took a little bit of charity with him.

But today he'd yet to walk by.

"Eva, can you ring up Mr. Miller?" Aunt Rhoda called from the kitchen, her apron thoroughly doused in flour and a disgruntled expression on her face.

Eva spun away from the window and took her place behind the register. "I apologize for my daydreaming," she said to her aunt and their patron.

The man laughed jovially. "Not to worry. You have a peaceful view out there today. All seems well with the world, doesn't it?"

Eva forced a smile in return. "I pray you're right, Mr. Miller."

"Believe me, I am. Did you hear? I got a job."

Eva paused and gave the man her full attention. Sam Miller was a Mennonite who had been out of work since he hurt his back last spring. He wasn't able to return to farming after his back surgery and had to depend on his wife and daughters to run the family farm without him. A sparkle she hadn't seen in his eyes for months brightened his face. How could she have missed it?

"This is wonderful news, Mr. Miller! Please, you must share where you will be working."

"It's not official yet. I'm meeting my new boss here today to discuss my responsibilities, but he's fairly certain I can handle the work, even with my limited physical capabilities."

"Will you start right away?"

"Ja, he's looking for me to jump right in. It seems he needs to leave town right away."

Eva, in the process of returning Mr. Miller's change, paused in midair. A sinking feeling tightened her throat and stopped her from asking any more questions about his new job.

The front door opened, ushering in a gust of cold air, and Jacob closed it quickly behind him. He stomped his boots on the rag rug and searched the seating area of the bakery.

"Over here, Mr. Wittmer," Sam Miller called from the register, accepting his change from Eva and pocketing it.

Eva didn't need to ask any more questions about where Sam would be working. She also didn't need to ask why the hurry.

Jacob would be leaving soon.

She'd known the day would arrive, but subconsciously she had tucked the thought away to face at a later date. Had the time come already?

Jacob approached the counter and said, "Good morning, Eva." His deep voice held some reserve.

Her throat remained tight, and all she could do was nod her greeting.

"Thank you for my fry pies each morning. I've looked forward to them."

"You're welcome," she managed to say. *I hoped you would come in and let me know you are okay. That* we *are okay.*

But those words didn't come.

"Shall we talk here, Sam?" Jacob nodded to an empty table by the bay window.

"Sounds great," Sam responded, leading the way and chatting with excitement.

Jacob followed and took a seat facing Eva.

He looked tired, with dark smudges beneath his eyes. She could tell he'd been working himself past his limit since she'd seen him last. All in order to get out of town faster—to get away from her.

Eva frowned and closed the register. What could she say to make him stop running?

"Eva, your sister's coming up the walk," Louisa called from the back kitchen.

Eva turned to the window in time to see Annie hide her cell phone in the secret pocket of her dress. Eva sighed at her sister's waywardness. She could only hope her Rumspringa would end soon. By the looks of it, though, not even the snow could slow Annie down.

Her sister rushed through the door, as gusty as the wind outside. "Wow, it's picking up," Annie announced, shaking the snowflakes from her shoulders. She peeked into the kitchen before sidling up to Eva and whispering, "Before the aunts come in, I want to tell you a secret."

Eva looked around to see that only one of the customers had noticed. She turned to block Annie from the view of the dining area. "What's going on?"

"I think I have a boyfriend."

"A boyfriend!"

All heads turned toward them.

"Shh!" Annie hissed, moving Eva away from prying eyes. "He's ex-Amish."

Eva inhaled. "You're asking for trouble. Mamm is going to be so upset."

"I didn't say I was getting married. I said I had a boyfriend. But he's not much of a boy. More like a man—like your Jacob."

"Shh!" Now it was Eva's turn to scold. "He's not *my* Jacob," Eva whispered as she jerked her head to warn her sister that he sat behind her.

Annie stood on her tiptoes and smiled. "He is so handsome. What's he doing here?"

"He's giving Mr. Miller a job."

Annie moved to cross the dining room.

"Annie, no!" But Eva's whisper went ignored.

"Hi, Mr. Miller. And . . . Jacob, right?" Annie asked. She touched a hand to Jacob's shoulder and Eva nearly choked. What was her sister doing? *Flirting?* Jacob wouldn't fall for that.

The smile he sent Annie's way said differently.

Eva could have sworn someone had sucker punched her. How foolish she'd been! To think he would look only at her that way was naive and childish. Hadn't she learned her lesson with Daniel? But that ache was nothing compared with the fact that this time it wasn't some strange Amish woman in another state. This time it was her sister.

Eva prayed for the jealous knot in her stomach to pass. She wanted no envy to come between them.

Besides, what did she expect? Annie was beautiful, with her fair, smooth skin and sleek blonde hair. Her blue eyes were filled with life and an excitement that made Eva wish she could run alongside her. What man wouldn't want Annie as his bride? Life promised adventure with her. With Eva, it promised the mundane.

Eva turned away and took out the vinegar-and-water solution she used to wash the counter. This was what she was *güt* at—cooking and cleaning. She rubbed the rag in circles across the glass top until it squeaked. Then she rubbed some more because cleaning was her outlet when she needed to work through something.

"Eva." Jacob spoke to her from behind, snapping her out of her melancholy. She made a few more circles with the rag before his hand covered hers, forcing her to stop. "I'd like to talk to you."

She stared at his hand. So strong yet so gentle. She could feel the calluses on the underside of his fingers pressing into her skin. He was a hard worker and it showed. Eva tried to be understanding, but it was difficult with him touching her, which she liked more than she cared to admit. His hand lingered on hers until she was forced to look him in the eyes.

"You shouldn't be behind the counter," she said harshly. Her choice of words dumbfounded her. Was this what jealousy did to a person? Made one petty? And yet she couldn't stop. "You're not allowed back here."

"I'll add it to the list of places I'm not allowed." Jacob didn't make a move. Not his hand, not even an eyelash. The smile he'd had for Annie was nowhere in sight. He searched Eva's face, from her eyes to her lips to her hair. Slowly a soft smile formed. "So beautiful," he whispered for only her to hear.

Eva swallowed hard, glancing toward the round windows in the swinging doors to see if her aunts were watching. They were busy rolling out cookie dough, their heads bent. Eva pulled her hand out of Jacob's, rubbing the place she still felt his touch. "Why would you say that?"

"Because you don't believe it. And it's true."

Eva touched her hair where her Kapp didn't cover it. "Well, thank you. That's kind of you to say."

Jacob shook his head, grinning. "Figures you would turn it around to compliment me."

"You were the one who said it."

"I will be careful not to do so in the future." His expression was deadpan.

Eva pursed her lips again, but this time she fought to keep a smile from breaking forth. "You're still behind my counter."

He laughed, a deep, robust sound she knew would garner inquisitive viewers. "I came back here to ask you a question. Remember?"

"Right, I'm sorry. How can I help you?"

"I'm about to hire Sam Miller to manage my shop. But before I do, I wanted to ask you what you think of my choice."

Eva angled a look behind Jacob's arm to see Sam and Annie chatting away. The man beamed with happiness. He looked like he was about to burst. "I think you've made a wonderful choice. Sam is a hard worker. Congratulations."

Eva looked back at Jacob. The smile he'd offered Annie was back, but there was something different in his eyes that hadn't been there when Annie approached him.

He was looking for her approval of his choice in a manager.

Jacob trusted her opinion.

Once again, Eva believed that Gött had sent this man to her to cover in prayer. He needed her, whether he wanted to admit it or not. And even if he fancied Annie over her, it didn't come close to the relationship he had already forged with her—one based on respect, trust, and honesty. If only she didn't feel a desperate ache when she thought of him leaving her life. Leaving her.

"Yes, Sam is a wonderful choice," she repeated with a nod of confirmation to his plea. Eva saw the tension ease from Jacob's broad shoulders.

"*Güt.*" He stepped away from her, leaving a void where the warmth of his presence had been. "Then I guess all I have left to do is hang the *Open for Business* sign."

Eva once again felt the air drain out of her. It seemed that the tension Jacob had just released had sunk into her shoulders.

Jacob was going, and there was nothing she could do about it.

Jacob stepped out the back entrance of the bakery and took a deep breath of fresh air. All week he'd rushed through the work to get his store up and running sooner than planned. After nearly kissing Eva at his shop, he'd thought it necessary to hightail it out of town for her sake.

He accepted an isolated future for himself, but he would never want that for her. Eva would make an amazing wife. She was wise beyond her years and knew how to run a business. Jacob hoped her future husband would look to Eva for guidance. She would bring a home of blessings upon him if he trusted her.

Even now, Jacob felt assured that Sam Miller was the man to run his store. It was more than his being Mennonite, not Old Order Amish, so he could handle the phone and computer orders. Jacob required more than that from the person who would be the face and voice of Amish-Crafted Furniture. Because he didn't know the people of the area, Jacob looked to Eva for her wisdom on the matter.

Telling her she was beautiful had slipped out, but he was glad it had. Eva might not believe it after being jilted. If Jacob could do anything for her before he left, he would make sure she knew the truth about herself.

Snowflakes grazed his lips. He touched his face and realized he was smiling.

A giggle told him he wasn't alone.

Annie's voice floated from across the parking lot. She stood over by his truck, talking on a cell phone. Jacob's smile changed to a frown. The teenager didn't understand the world. She only saw opportunities to run free without consequence.

Except there were always consequences. Maybe none so drastic as his had been, but any consequence would be painful. Jacob had a feeling Eva would take the brunt of her sister's penalties. He'd seen them together only a couple of times, but Eva seemed to shelter and care for the younger woman.

Jacob neared Annie, his boots silent through the powdery snow.

"I can go tonight, Peter," she said into her phone.

The name *Peter* stopped Jacob short. He immediately shook off his unease as silly. His cousin Peter was in another state, far from here, far enough away to keep Jacob safe from exposure.

Still, Jacob wished he could hear the voice on the other end. Was this the boyfriend he'd overheard Annie telling Eva about? Was he Amish?

Jacob cleared his throat to make himself known.

Annie whipped around. Slowly her surprise turned into a sly smile.

Jacob took a step back.

"I need to go," she said into the phone. "I have a friend here. I'll see you later." Annie pocketed the phone.

"Your boyfriend?" Jacob asked.

"You jealous?" She tilted her head, but the look on her face didn't sit right with him, no matter how pretty she was. She moved in closer to him.

Jacob held his ground.

The tips of their boots touched.

Annie lifted her chin and looked at his lips. "You really are extremely handsome. I don't know why Eva hasn't claimed you." Her eyes narrowed. "Or has she, and you turned her down?"

"That's not fair or kind. It's also none of your concern, and I think you should take a few steps back. Someone may look out the window and see you."

"Us, you mean." She stayed put.

"Annie, I don't think you understand the fire you are playing with. You shouldn't be cavorting with the ways of the world. Trust me. Step away and go home."

Daggers flared in her eyes. "You have no right to tell me what to do."

"I am only thinking of your well-being and your sister's heart, which would be grieved to see you like this."

"Watch this." Annie leaned in to kiss him.

Jacob stiffened for the impact, but it never came. Annie stopped a breath away from his lips, then pulled back.

Güt, the girl had some sense left in her. She wasn't a lost cause.

Jacob looked around to make sure no one had witnessed the event. A few cars were parked in the lot, but he didn't see anyone watching. That didn't mean there weren't eyes on them.

He turned to walk away but said over his shoulder, "I suggest you learn to find contentment in your Amish community, Annie. Don't run too freely. Make better choices before it's too late for you too."

7

As Eva was putting Jacob's apple fry pie in its box the next morning, her Mamm and Daed opened the back door and stepped inside.

"*Gute Mariye. Wie bischt du?*" Mamm said cheerfully as she wiped her boots on the mat and removed her gloves.

Rhoda and Louisa stopped their work to welcome their younger brother and his wife with open arms. "We are well. How are you? Ready for Christmas?"

"That's why we came to town this morning. We had a few errands to run and thought we would come in for a cup of *Kaffe*."

Eva went to the stove to pour her parents two cups. When she turned back with the steaming cups in her hands, she noticed Mamm eyeing the small box on the counter.

"Putting together orders, Eva?"

Coffee sloshed over the sides of the cups in Eva's hands. Lying to her mother wasn't an option. Eva didn't think she ever remembered even trying it, and she wasn't about to start now. She glanced in her aunts' direction, hoping for some help.

Both suddenly had important tasks to handle and avoided eye contact.

Eva placed the cups of coffee down in front of her parents. "Not technically. That box is for the tenant upstairs. He likes fry pies, so I made one for him."

A *humph* came from one of her aunts.

"I mean, I set one aside for him from the batch I made today." Eva shot a pointed look at her aunts.

"I think that's nice of you," Mamm said, then turned to Daed. "Don't you?"

Eva's father wasn't so quick to reply. He stroked his beard and looked to the back staircase. For a moment, Eva feared her Daed might call Jacob down, but finally he said, "I suppose it's neighborly."

Eva relaxed enough to continue with Jacob's box, but she had second thoughts about the ribbon. She put on her cloak to deliver the box to his doorstep before he left for the furniture shop.

"When you take Jacob his fry pie," Mamm said, "be sure to tell him he is more than welcome to come to our home for Christmas dinner. He should not celebrate alone, and we would love to have him."

Eva paused at the door, wanting to run into her mother's arms and thank her.

But Rhoda interrupted and said, "The man might not be here for Christmas. I see he opened his shop, so he'll be on his way soon."

Her mother frowned at Eva. "That's too bad."

"It's just as well," Rhoda said without looking up from her work.

Eva worried that she might mention the newspaper article to her parents. She silently pleaded with her not to.

"Why do you say that?" Mamm asked.

Rhoda shrugged, glancing at Eva. "I just figured he would want to be home with his family, that's all."

"I'm sure that's true. But do tell him he is welcome if he isn't able to be home in time."

Eva nodded and opened the door.

Her mother stopped her once again. "Have you seen Annie? I don't think she came home last night."

Her sister could be so thoughtless. "No, Mamm, but I'm sure I will. I'll tell her to get home."

"Denki. I know she's having fun, but I do worry."

Eva hastily departed before her mother could see the anger on her face. Eva would tell Annie a lot more than *go home* when she saw her. As she made it around the back of the building, the door to the private entrance of Jacob's apartment opened.

Eva halted on the shoveled path. She was delivering his box later than she had the previous days.

Jacob closed the door behind him and stared at her for a quiet moment. He glanced at the box and said, "You spoil me, Eva. You're also going to make me *fett*."

"It has fruit in it. That makes it healthy, right?"

He laughed and walked over to take the box. "I have to admit, I have enjoyed opening my door each morning to your sweet gifts, and when I didn't see the box this morning, I was a little let down. But here you are. The gift is better with the gift bearer, for sure."

Eva wanted to ask him when he planned to leave, but the words wouldn't come. "How's the store?" she asked instead.

"Coming along. My team is getting the hang of taking orders, and I'm starting to feel comfortable with them being on their own."

So, does that mean a few days or a few weeks?

"Mamm invited you to Christmas dinner at our home, if you're still here." Eva blurted it out faster than she intended, but it was the only way—like ripping a bandage off. Let him tell her now and get it over with.

"That's nice of her, but I don't think it's a wise decision."

"Because you won't be here?"

"No, I probably will still be here. It's for other reasons. But thank you. I need to get going now—to pick up some supplies." Jacob headed toward his truck. "And thank you for the apple fry pie."

"Is it because of what happened in Indiana with the young woman who died?"

Jacob froze, his eyes wide with shock. Another bandage had just been ripped off. Confronting him like this was not how she had wanted to bring it up.

"My aunts . . ." Eva cleared her throat and tried again. "They're concerned because of an article in the paper about you."

Jacob nodded. "I see." He stared at his truck.

"You don't need to be worried. We don't think any less of you. I know you've been shunned, and it's not only for leaving your community but for some other event that happened in your district. I would like to help you reconcile with your community. I could speak—"

"No." Jacob stopped her. "I don't want you involving yourself in my personal matters. I don't want you talking to anyone about me."

"But don't you see? You could be free to return to your home. You could be free to marry."

"Is that what this is about? Marriage?" Jacob's voice rose, but he quickly took a breath and calmed down. "My days in Indiana are long gone. There is no going back—ever. There's also no going forward for me. No home. No marriage."

Eva took a step toward him, her hand outstretched toward his. Would he take it?

Slowly Jacob turned his hand so his fingers could entwine with hers. They stood in silence, staring at how their hands fit comfortably into each other's.

But his words were far from comforting.

"Eva, you need to accept that there is no hope for a future with me. Don't tell me you haven't thought about it. I'd be lying if I said I haven't thought about it too, and for that, I am sorry. But it needs to stop. Right now. I plan to leave after Christmas, but if you can't let this idea go, I will need to leave sooner, for both our sakes."

"Are you done? Because I would like to speak too." Eva pulled her hand away.

"Go ahead."

"I wasn't referring to marrying you. I was talking about you looking forward to a future with someone, anyone. Not me."

"Not you, huh?"

"No, of course not. I would never—"

"You would never marry me?"

"That's not what I was going to say. I would never be so bold as to—"

"Tell me." Jacob frowned. The fight had clearly flown out of him. "I'm sorry for doing this to you. For putting you in this situation. I think it's best if I leave early after all. Besides, your aunts can't be too excited to have me under their roof, now that they know of my past."

Eva thought of Rhoda's words a few minutes ago. Having him in the apartment did bother them. "We really don't know much, only that a young woman died before you left. She fell?"

The question hung between them.

Then Jacob scoffed, a challenging look on his face. "Don't you really want to ask me if I killed her?"

A tremor raced through Eva's body. "I don't believe you could do such a thing."

He leaned in and said, "You should."

Could she be wrong about him? The thought was like a burn from a hot oven.

Jacob turned to his truck. He slammed the door in his wake before speeding out of the lot.

The bakery's door opened for the fiftieth time since Jacob's hasty and disturbing retreat that morning. Eva welcomed the customer with a smile she knew was unconvincing. She went through the motions of handling the order, waiting for the bell to jingle again.

Jacob had to return to explain what he meant about her not believing him guilty of such a heinous crime. *Why does he want me to think him capable of murder?* Eva imagined his strong, hardworking hands taking a life. She rubbed her hand where he had held her so gently and couldn't fathom it.

Because it's not true.

For whatever reason, Jacob wanted her to believe the worst of him, but she wouldn't do it. She would continue to stand by him, even when everyone else didn't.

Eva glanced through the circle windows to see her aunts working. The ladies were having serious doubts about letting Jacob remain upstairs, Rhoda especially. The way she'd nearly mentioned the newspaper to Eva's parents this morning showed that the secret weighed on her. She probably feared someone would soon learn how they knew about his past and question her about why she hadn't revealed what she knew.

More important, what would their decision to rent to Jacob do to their business, their livelihood? Eva hadn't worried about her aunts' bakery until Jacob told her she should consider him guilty. If Jacob had killed someone and was on the run, renting to him could shut her aunts' business down. Eva had to be sure her aunts didn't get hurt because they'd decided to trust her.

Because she'd decided to trust him.

Please, Jacob, come back and fix this before it's too late.

Eva bent down to move the pastries from the bottom rack to the higher shelf. The door jingled, and she looked up from behind the counter to see if it was Jacob.

Bishop Roy Swartzentruber stood in the doorway, searching the room.

Eva straightened up. "Hello, Bishop. What can I do for you? Do you want my aunts?"

"No, Eva. I'm here to speak to you about Jacob Wittmer."

Eva looked around the room to see the three other customers eating and chatting at their tables. She pointed to a table in the back corner. "Would you like to sit?"

"This won't take long." He reached into his pocket and withdrew a cell phone.

Stunned, she waited for him to explain why he would have a cell phone.

"Do you recognize this phone?"

Eva remembered seeing a phone like it. Was it Annie's? "Should I?" she asked.

"I think we both know who it belongs to. I found it last night in the parking lot when I came to town to run some errands for my wife. You know how she loves your bread. I thought I would pick her up a loaf."

"I'm glad to hear that, but what does this phone have to do with Jacob?"

Bishop frowned. "It was near his private entrance. I saw it as I passed by his door."

Jacob's entrance? Why would Annie's phone be near Jacob's door? Unless . . .

Eva caught sight of the kitchen doors opening wide behind the bishop. Her aunts stood in the doorway with fear on their faces. They believed the worst of Jacob, and if there was something going on with him and Annie, they would be right to do so.

Whole scenarios of Jacob and Annie together played out in her mind. She prayed they didn't play on her face. "It could be a customer's," she said unconvincingly.

The bishop nodded, his straight, short beard moving in stiff unison. He placed the phone in her hand, pressing it against her palm. "I pray it is. And I hope you find its owner."

"Denki." Another lame response.

The bishop donned his black hat, tipping it to the aunts as he left, and closed the door behind him with a soft *click*.

The aunts locked gazes on Eva.

"We can't hide this any longer," Rhoda said. "This is no longer a matter of the heart. There is something going on, and someone's going to get hurt."

8

Jacob took another turn in his apartment. He looked at the clock, waiting for the hour hand to hit five o'clock. Five more minutes until the bakery's closing time. He had so much to say to Eva. Leaving things as he had this morning felt disgraceful. She should tell him his apology was empty, yet he hoped she wouldn't. He hoped for so much more, even when more would never be possible.

Eva only knew the half of it.

She knew the basics of Lily's death. She knew what the paper said about him. But she didn't know the truth about the role he'd played in it all. Only two people knew the truth.

And one of them was dead.

Jacob tapped his foot in a rapid cadence. The clock's ticking didn't speed up to match.

A soft knock on his private entrance door downstairs pulled his attention away. He stayed put, unsure if he wanted company now.

The knock came again, a bit louder. "Jacob? It's Eva."

Jacob raced to the stairwell and bounded down, skipping stairs to reach the door in record time. He pulled it open wide. "Please, please forgive me. I—I don't deserve it, I know."

The tortured expression on Eva's sweet face nearly undid him. She looked beyond him to the stairway. "Is Annie here?"

Her question left him dumbfounded. Then he remembered Annie's attempt to kiss him the day before. Had Eva witnessed it from the bakery window?

If so, he had so much more to make right with this woman.

"I wouldn't put your sister in such an immoral situation. I wouldn't do that to anybody. You must believe me—"

"I do," she interrupted him. "You're an honorable man, Jacob. I know that." Her gaze dropped to something in her hand. She opened her palm to reveal a cell phone. "It's Annie's. Bishop found it here by your door yesterday."

So she hadn't seen the exchange with Annie. Jacob nearly fell back against the wall in relief, grateful that the honorable ideas she had of him were still intact. Even after he had alluded to killing Lily. Not that he should want her to think he was honorable. He was leaving.

Then the fact that Annie's phone was found by his door—and found by Bishop Roy—sank in. Jacob's short-lived relief evaporated as he surmised what this new finding would lead to.

"All I can say is I don't know why this was found by my door. She must have dropped it, or it fell out of her pocket."

Eva nodded with a thoughtful expression. "She made a secret pocket inside her dress. She's so sneaky right now."

"The fact that it was Bishop Roy who brought this to you must hurt." At her nod, he continued, "I know the plain life means everything to you, and you wish it was the same for Annie."

Eva raised her chin, looking ready to say something drastic.

"What is it, Eva? What do you want to say?"

She sighed and hesitated, then asked, "Do you like my sister?"

Jacob jerked. "Um, sure, she's nice."

"No, I mean do you *like* her? As in courting. I know she's so much more worldly than I am and so much prettier—"

"Stop." Jacob reached for her hand and raised his other hand to her cheek. The softness of her cherublike face struck him. He rubbed his thumb tenderly down its side to her jaw, where he lifted her chin to look him straight in the eyes. "Don't ever compare your beauty to someone else's. They will lose hands down every time."

Eva's green eyes liquefied before him, and her lips parted on a sharp inhale.

The urge to kiss her overpowered every part of Jacob, deafening him to the part that knew there was no future for them. "You are the most beautiful woman I have ever seen. I love the color of your hair and your eyes. I love the smile that you offer so freely. I love the way you bring light into the dark places of my life. I love your sense of decency and order that makes your beauty shine through. I love your view of the world around you and the people you meet. You lift me up with words of encouragement, and I see you do the same for all your customers. They leave your bakery standing taller than when they entered, and it's all because of you. Believe me, Eva, I wish to Gött you were mine. Not Annie. You."

Eva's eyes widened and filled with tears again. "You wish I was yours?" she squeaked out.

He'd gone too far. Jacob dropped his hands and stepped back, trying to regroup from the direction of this conversation. "I'm sorry. I was too forward, especially when my life is not mine to give."

"You don't understand." Eva rushed forward, filling the gap between them again. She grabbed his forearm, scrunching the fabric of his sleeve. She seemed almost desperate to share what was on her mind. And yet she didn't seem able to speak.

"What is it? You can tell me anything." He wished he could be as honest with her.

Her smile slowly grew as she visibly relaxed. "Before you arrived I prayed for you, an honorable man, a traveler."

"You've said this. I already told you I don't—"

"Wait. There's more." She swallowed so hard that he could hear her gulp. "I had the same wish," she whispered. "You wished for me to be yours, and I—I wished for you to be mine."

"Eva!" Aunt Rhoda called from the back door of the bakery. "Where are you?"

Eva's hand froze on Jacob's arm.

He nearly pulled her inside to finish their conversation. He had so much he wanted to say. Instead he told her, "Go. Go back to your family. It's best this way."

"No." Eva bit her lower lip. "I don't see how this could ever be better."

"Eva!" Aunt Rhoda called again.

"Take this and hide it." Eva shoved the cell phone into his palm. "Coming!" And with that, she turned in a swirl of her skirt and cloak and scurried around the side of the building.

Jacob leaned back against the wall and took his first deep breath since she'd told him her wish.

"Your smile is infectious, Eva," Mamm called from the wraparound porch of their two-story home.

"I didn't realize I was smiling," Eva replied, as she crunched through the packed snow on the walkway.

"I'd say putting the horse away made you happy, but I watched you all the way down the lane, and that smile was there then too. Will you share?"

Eva ran up the stairs into her mother's waiting arms. "You saw me coming down the lane. How long have you been out here? And why, when I know you have so much to do?"

When she didn't respond, Eva pulled back and watched her mother's serene expression contort into sudden sadness. "What's wrong? What's happened?"

"Nothing to pay any mind to. I'm sure all is *güt*."

Eva didn't budge. She stared at Mamm, silently waiting for the truth—even as it came to her in an instant. "It's Annie, isn't it? She's done something to bring shame on herself and us."

Her mother's frown told Eva she had hit the nail on the head.

"Where is she?" As Eva recollected, she hadn't seen Annie since she stopped by the bakery two days ago. But with Annie skipping out at night and still gone when Eva left for work, it wasn't impossible they'd missed each other in passing.

"I don't know where she is," Mamm answered. "Your Daed says we need to accept that Annie has chosen the Englisch world over ours."

Eva inhaled sharply at such a thought. It was inconceivable. Why would she? *How* could she? "I don't believe it. Annie wouldn't leave us. Not for good. Not without saying goodbye. She told me—"

"She said goodbye," Mamm said quietly, cutting her off. "I didn't realize when she said it to me that it was final. I wish I had. I would have held her a little while longer."

"There must be an explanation. I'll find her. I promise I'll bring her home."

"Eva, you made your choice. You must let your sister make hers now."

"But she didn't say goodbye," Eva repeated. "Not to me. She didn't say goodbye to me."

The front door opened, and her Daed stood on the other side. The stern face that instilled fear in many only gave Eva a solid foundation to stand on. He offered protection to his family. He offered order and safety. "Eva, come inside," he instructed.

But for the first time in her life, Eva didn't want to obey. She wanted to go look for Annie. "Please, Daed, let me go find her."

"You heard your Mamm. You are forbidden to look for her. She's made her choice. All we can do is pray she decides to repent and come home. Everyone is given the same opportunity to decide. She's made hers."

Eva gazed at the windows on the porch. Each pane of glass shone brightly with a single candle behind it—a symbol of the Christ Child to the lost and weary. She turned to face the road and lifted a silent prayer for Annie to see the lights and come home.

She was forbidden to look for her sister, but somehow she had to figure out a way to get around the command. She would never disobey her father, so how could she find Annie?

Later, as Eva set the table for dinner, her mind ran with possibilities. One way included a certain man who had put the smile on her face today. Would Jacob help her deceive her father?

Eva hated even asking him. After she'd prayed so fervently for an honorable man, here she was, contemplating asking him to compromise his values for her. How could she ask such a thing?

"You forgot Annie's place setting," Daed said in an emotionless voice.

Eva placed a plate by Annie's chair. For the rest of her life, Annie would know there was a place set for her at a table. That somewhere in her past, she had left behind a family who would always set a place for her. It was a powerful tie to her home, especially when Annie found herself cold and alone in the Englisch world. When she found herself lost in a strange city, she would look out at the electric lights and remember the candlelight in the windows of her home in Blossom Creek. She would remember that her place at her family's table was waiting for her and would call her home.

Or so Eva hoped.

9

The furniture shop buzzed with the sound of earnest labor. The smell of freshly cut oak filled Jacob's senses but also his pride. His finished floor model pieces, furniture with clean lines and sturdy joints, were positioned around the showroom, ready for customers to view and order for their homes. There was only one piece of business left for him to handle before he could turn the operation over to Sam and Luke. He needed to finish the front desk.

Jacob's employees were working together in the back workshop on their first order, a dining room table and chairs. Jacob wanted them to complete the order before Christmas, so he'd opted to complete the desk himself. It wasn't as though he had a place to be for the holiday. It would be just another day for him. Unless he accepted Eva's invitation—then it would be something amazing. Did he dare believe it was possible?

Jacob swiped a hand along the half-completed front desk. He envisioned it finished. A mental image of Eva sitting behind the desk, helping him work, took over his mind. He held back a blink to prolong the image.

What would it be like to have a family-owned business where his wife was an integral part, working with him side by side?

Wife.

First she's sitting behind the desk and now she's my wife? The woman had infiltrated his life, slipping through his defenses as though she had the key.

Jacob closed his eyes and pinched the bridge of his nose at the absurdity. Absurd because of who he was. No, he didn't dare hope for any of it. He opened his eyes and, as if on cue, Eva stood on the other side of the window, looking in.

Her pale cheeks, rosy with the cold, her green eyes . . . red from weeping?

The next moment Jacob burst out his storefront door, reaching for her. He didn't care who looked on or what they might think. All he cared about was what had made Eva cry.

"Are you hurt?" he asked in a rush, his boots skidding to a stop before the tips of hers. His rough hands grabbed hold of the tops of her shoulders in a grip he barely controlled.

"Only in here." She touched the place over her heart as more tears spilled down her cheeks. She tried to turn away from him, but the attempt proved futile. "I shouldn't have come."

"Always, Eva. Tell me what you need. Let me help you."

"Do you mean that? Will you help me?" He felt the last of her resolve give way as she leaned toward him.

"After you showed so much belief in me, of course. What is it?"

Her lips quivered as her gaze dropped to her ungloved hands. "Annie ran away. No one has seen her since Monday. She's left us, and I've been forbidden to search for her."

Eva's announcement caught him off guard. "Who has forbidden you? Your Daed?"

"And Bishop."

Jacob looked down the street one way, then the other. He knew instantly what she wanted of him. "You want to disobey an order from your bishop, and you need my help?"

"It's for Annie. She needs me. I know she does. She would never have left without saying goodbye."

Jacob had different ideas about who Annie Stoltz was, and they weren't as noble as Eva's. But to say so to a woman in mourning would do no good. Still, he had to share his thoughts for Eva's good. "Let me walk you back to the bakery."

She didn't move but searched his face. "You're not going to help me, are you?"

"How would I help you find her?"

"You have connections to the Englisch world. You have a phone in your store. It would be acceptable for you to talk to Sheriff Murphy. Bishop hasn't asked you not to."

"He wouldn't ask me, because he would expect you to obey his request." Jacob raised a hand to hold off the objection forming on her lips. "Hear me out. You have proven to your community that you belong with them and the plain lifestyle. You have given your life to Gött and have vowed to follow His commandments. Bishop trusts you."

Heartbreak usurped Eva's expression. His words reached her even without him having to bring Annie's decisions into the conversation. There was no reason to cause her more pain, especially pain she couldn't control. Annie's choices were hers alone, even if those choices affected others.

Jacob nearly said he would go after Annie, if only to give her a talking-to. How dare she leave Eva and her family this close to Christmas? The girl needed a severe lesson from the school of hard knocks.

But who was he to be giving lessons on responsibility? He had run from his as well.

Jacob pushed his own faults aside for the woman before him. "I wish I could help you."

"More wishes," she mumbled. "I'm beginning to doubt if wishes ever do come true." With that, she turned abruptly and stepped out on the street before he could stop her.

A car slammed on its horn and nearly clipped her.

Eva didn't miss a step, keeping up her pace to the other side of the street.

Jacob called out to her and started to walk down his side of the street, his gaze following her. "Eva, stop! Don't go away like this."

"Hey, Jacob," Luke called after him from the shop. "Sam says you have a phone call."

Jacob took his gaze from Eva to look at Luke. "Can he take a message?"

"He says it's urgent," Luke answered.

Jacob watched Eva run inside the bakery, then turned back to his store. "Do you know who it is?"

"No, Sam said he didn't give a name. He just asked for you and said he'd wait. But it's an Indiana phone number. Maybe it's someone from your town."

Luke's words slowed Jacob's steps, but he made his way back, where Sam handed him the phone and stepped away to give him privacy.

Jacob put the phone to his ear. "This is Jacob Wittmer."

"There you are, Jacob. I was beginning to think you weren't going to take my call."

Peter. Peter Güngerich.

"How did you find me?" Jacob asked.

"Find you? You're my cousin. I've always known where you are."

A fast replay of all the towns Jacob traveled through in the past six years unwound in his mind. He'd been so careful to leave a complex trail behind him, but had Peter known anyway?

"How?" was the only thing Jacob could say.

"Don't worry about all that. What's important is that I want you to come home."

"*You* want me to come home? Just you?"

Silence followed and Jacob had his answer.

"What's this about, Peter? Why are you really calling me? Why have you kept track of my whereabouts all these years? I want the truth."

"I'm sure you do," he said smugly. Then a spark of anger came through the phone. "Look, it's been six years. You left and have gotten on with your life, but I haven't been able to."

"Gotten on with my life? Are you kidding? I live on the run."

"Then stop running and come home. Tell the truth about what took place that night at the farm. I want to follow in my Daed's footsteps as bishop, but the elders won't give me the time of day as long as some of them harbor doubts of what really happened to Lily."

"And what was that? What really happened to Lily?"

"Come on, Jacob. You know she jumped. She committed suicide and we both know it."

"I don't know any such thing. All I saw was her lying dead on the floor of the silo and you up above saying she jumped."

Peter let go an expletive before lashing out. "I can't believe you're not tired of this yet. You can fix this."

"I can fix this for *you*, you mean. I left town and took the blame with me. That's all I'm doing for you. Honestly I hope they never ordain you as bishop. I have my doubts about you too."

More silence ensued. Jacob thought Peter had hung up and nearly did the same.

But then a deep, malicious voice came over the line. "Your new girlfriend is cute. You should come home, or she might get hurt. I'd hate to see her end up like Lily."

The line went dead.

Slowly Jacob brought the phone down to the sideboard and let it clatter back into the cradle.

The buzz saw had ceased its noise, and Sam and Luke stood in the doorway at the back.

"Is everything all right?" Luke asked.

"I—I have to go. I have to leave town."

"I thought you were staying through Christmas," Sam said. "I mean, if you have to, we can handle things, of course, but Eva . . ." Sam's discomfort showed. Jacob had been kidding himself if he thought the whole town didn't see the way he and Eva looked at each other. They were all expecting an announcement any day now.

More reason to leave before Christmas.

But nothing as dire as a threat on her life if he stayed. Would Peter really hurt Eva? Jacob had asked that same question for years about Lily.

Judging by Peter's actions today, Jacob had no more doubts. Peter had been hitting Lily, and Jacob did nothing to help her. She had committed suicide to escape a marriage of abuse—or Peter had killed her to shut her up.

Either way, Eva was now being threatened by the same man, and Jacob had to do whatever it took to keep her safe.

"Where will you go?" Sam asked.

"Just tell Eva goodbye for me." Jacob grabbed his keys from the hook on the wall and his coat from the rack. "Tell her it's for the best."

Eva held her prayer box in her hands. The single slip of paper with its foolish wish still rested inside. Making a second wish for Annie's return seemed just as foolish when there was no way Eva could go looking for her. But Eva still had to try.

"Aunt Louisa, I'm going to take my prayer box and go for a walk to the barn, if that's all right with you."

"Of course, child. You could use some devotional time. It's slow this afternoon, and Aunt Rhoda will be back shortly from the deliveries. Why don't you hitch up Keepsake and go on home? You can pray while you drive."

Aunt Louisa picked a pie off the shelf and wrapped it in a checkered cloth. "Take this to my *Brudder*. Enjoy it after your dinner." She handed it to Eva after she'd put on her cloak. A kiss on the cheek followed, then Aunt Louisa's warm hand. She patted Eva's cheek gently. "Smile. We hate to see you so sad. I know you miss Annie, but we must go on. A life of diligence and responsibility is our way."

"I know. Annie made her choice, but it just doesn't make sense. She told me she had no plans to leave the community."

Louisa frowned. "Boys have a way of changing a girl's mind. And we know there was someone she fancied. She said so herself. She'll come home when the shine dims."

"I wish I knew who he was and how to find him."

"Nonsense," Louisa scolded. "You will do as your family and Bishop said. No searching for her, only praying for her return. If it is Gött's will, she will come back to us."

A horse neighed outside, signaling someone was arriving in the lot. "Jacob said the same thing. I must obey the order given."

"Eva, you didn't ask him to find Annie for you, I hope."

Eva dropped her gaze to her prayer box. "I'm sorry. I know I shouldn't have but—"

The back door opened to reveal Rhoda had returned from the deliveries. The sisters shared a moment of some sort of silent communication Eva didn't understand.

Rhoda gave a nod before going about the business of hanging up her coat and scarf. "What are the two of you talking about?" she asked as she straightened her Kapp.

There was no sense withholding the conversation. Louisa would tell her sister anyway. Eva confessed, "I asked Jacob to help me find Annie."

Rhoda's face paled. "What have you done?" Her usually sweet tone turned cold and disappointed.

"He said no. Don't worry. He won't do it."

"He said no?" Rhoda's disbelief mirrored Eva's original thoughts.

"It's just as I've been saying since the day he arrived in Blossom Creek. Jacob Wittmer is a *güt* man. He knows following Bishop's orders is the right thing to do. I'm the one who failed when I asked him. And before you give me a lecture, I'm off to make amends with Gött."

"Ach," Louisa said, wringing her hands, "I think we've made a mistake."

The sisters continued their silent conversation again, but this time pointed looks became etched worry accentuating their aged wrinkles. Rhoda plopped herself on the stool with a deep sigh.

"What's wrong?" Eva asked. "Has something happened that you're not telling me?"

Louisa stood by her sister, the two stronger together as always. "I think we made a bad choice about young Jacob Wittmer. He does seem to be an honorable man, despite what the newspaper said about him. Still, you should know the bishop may send him away."

"I don't understand," Eva said. She suddenly remembered the look Rhoda gave Louisa when she returned and the nod that passed between them. "What have you done?"

Louisa placed a hand on her sister's shoulder, offering comfort and support.

Rhoda said, "I gave Bishop the newspaper."

"Why?" Both women jumped when Eva cried out. Eva backed away from the two women she had trusted with every part of her life.

"Eva, please understand. The secrecy was creating conflict in my soul." Tears filled Rhoda's eyes. "When Bishop came by to ask about

Jacob, I thought we were wrong about the man. That you were wrong about him. I'm sorry. But now you tell us how he turned you down when you asked him to help you defy an order. If only I'd known earlier."

Louisa added, "When I see Bishop, I will tell him how Jacob wanted you to honor his order. It will speak in his favor. I know it will. Please forgive us."

Eva wished Rhoda hadn't given the paper to Bishop, but she also knew that secrecy was not the Amish way. She understood her aunts' choice had been intended for her good, even if it had been in error. For fear of saying something hurtful, Eva remained quiet but offered them a nod to indicate that she forgave them.

Eva made her way to the barn. She knew her aunts watched her from the bakery window. Keepsake nickered when Eva brought the reins down on her and hitched her to the black buggy.

"Good girl, Keepsake. Always ready and willing to take my lead. I should follow your ways."

As they moved out of the barn, Eva turned her thoughts heavenward. *Please, Lord Gött, forgive me for going against Bishop. Forgive my childish ways. Help me forgive Louisa and Rhoda with no animosity between us. They are everything to me. I know they thought they were protecting me.*

The buggy moved down the street in an unhurried way. Eva opened her prayer box on the seat and read the slip of paper still inside.

I wish for this honorable man to be mine.

Jacob had wished for the same from her. Both of them were foolish in their wishes. Eva reached for the paper, planning to throw it out, but just then she passed the Amish-Crafted Furniture store. The lights were on, but Jacob's truck was gone.

Has he gone to look for Annie after all?

A sick feeling swept over Eva. If he had, it was because of her. She had no one else to blame.

The county line fast approached as Jacob sped farther away from Blossom Creek. He shot a glimpse in his rearview mirror, expecting to hear sirens at any minute, just as he'd expected on the night he'd fled his own community.

But no person chased him down.

Only his past did.

The same past that would forever be chasing him, no matter where he went or what he did. Going home to Indiana could never be an option.

But was running for the rest of his life the answer?

Jacob was leaving town to keep Eva safe, but how safe was she, even with him on the run in another state or another country?

What if Peter took his vengeance out on Eva anyway?

Jacob slammed on his brakes, and his truck skidded to a screeching halt. He glanced in the mirror again. The wide-open road back to Blossom Creek beckoned.

"No more running," he said aloud. "That road ends here."

Jacob cranked the steering wheel to the left and drove over the median that separated the freeway. He gave his truck the gas it needed to propel him back to Blossom Creek. Back to Eva.

Lord, I know I haven't come to You in a long time, but I need Your help. I should have come to You when I knew Lily wasn't safe, but I didn't. I took matters into my own hands, and I will regret that decision for the rest of my life. He sighed.

But now, Eva is in danger. Help me to do the right thing this time. Help me to keep her safe from a madman—from a killer. I know I don't have the proof to say such a thing about Peter, but it doesn't matter. I know, deep down, he is a murderer. Guide my steps. Eva says You led her to pray for me even before I came to Blossom Creek. If that is true, then I ask You to guide my steps again. Lead me to where I need to go.

As Jacob drove on, his snow tires crunching on pavement was the only sound. It became a white noise that offered solace for where he was headed.

He took the exit for Blossom Creek, but when he came to the intersection that would lead to Main Street, he didn't take it. Instead he turned the wheel toward the country roads that were beginning to feel comfortable.

He passed an Amish homestead. Smoke billowed from the chimneys, and soft candlelight glowed from the windows. He envied the family that lived there as he drove on.

A familiar fence loomed ahead, and Jacob slowed down to take the turn into the drive. An enclosed black buggy sat out front, a horse still tied to the reins.

Jacob pulled up next to it and stepped out of his truck. Someone else was visiting as well. It was probably not the right time to make this call, but then, there never would be a good time.

Jacob walked up the front steps and onto the large porch. He wiped sweaty hands on his jeans and took a deep breath. Lifting a fist, he gave three quick knocks.

Heavy footsteps thudded across wood floors and grew louder as they neared. A lock clicked, and the door opened wide.

Bishop Roy Swartzentruber stood stolid and severe on the other side of the threshold. The smiling bishop was gone. This was not the same man who had invited him to a cordial lunch. This man had business to handle that would not go smoothly for Jacob.

"Bishop, I'm here to ask for your guidance."

"Güt, because I plan to give it. I know who you are, Jacob Wittmer—who you *really* are. How you are to blame for the death of a young bride and why you ran from your punishment. I will not turn you in, but you are to move out of the Stoltzes' apartment by tomorrow morning. You are to leave our quiet and respectable community alone. I can't make you leave town or close your business, but you can be sure the Amish of Blossom Creek will not be patrons."

"Sir, please, there's something you don't know. It's about Eva. Do with me as you see fit, but Eva—"

"Eva Stoltz is not your concern. I forbid the two of you to be together. Now get off my property."

Bishop Roy shut the door quietly, not with the slam Jacob had been expecting.

For the elder of a community, self-control was a key value to have. Jacob made his way back to his truck, thinking the man might have forgotten that listening was a crucial part of the job too.

Jacob climbed in and started the engine. *Now where to, Lord? Because the first stop just made everything worse. How am I supposed to protect Eva if I can't even be near her?*

10

"Bishop has spoken," Aunt Rhoda explained through the roaring in Eva's head. "There is naught for us to do."

"Is he gone?" Eva whispered. She had just learned she was to have no contact with Jacob again. "Has he moved out? Is that why I didn't see his truck in the parking lot?"

"It would appear so." Louisa lit the stoves and stood erect, blowing out the match. "I don't think he even stayed here last night. That man is certainly obedient to the elders."

Eva jumped up from the stool. "That has to count for something, don't you think? Will you talk to Bishop and explain?"

Louisa frowned, tying on her apron. "Of course we will, but Bishop doesn't lift ordinances at the drop of a hat. I know this pains you, but I think you need to accept that Jacob will never be a part of your life. There's just too much unknown from his past to have anything solid to build on."

"Solid? What about Gött and His plan for Jacob?"

"We know you believe the Lord led Jacob to our door, and maybe He did, but that doesn't mean He meant for the two of you to be together."

"You asked me to pray for my heart's desire. Remember that?"

Rhoda sighed and looked at her sister. They both nodded.

"When I prayed for a man of integrity and honesty to live upstairs, I also made a wish. I wished for that noble man to be mine."

Before they could dampen her confession with reason, Eva continued, "And Aunts, Jacob has also wished for me to be his."

At their sharp inhales, Eva knew she might have crossed the line with Louisa and Rhoda. They could go to her Daed and tell him what she had shared with them. If they did so, it would be out of concern for her, but it would still feel like broken trust. It could even ruin the atmosphere they had built here at the bakery.

"I only share this with you because I want you to know who Jacob Wittmer is," Eva explained. "The Jacob I know cares for me, but he will put his wants aside for my well-being. I asked him to help me find Annie, and he turned me down, not because he didn't want to help me but because he cared about what would happen to me. I would have been shunned, and he protected me from that. He protected me from my own poor choices."

The aunts began pulling down the flour and prepping for the bread.

It seemed to Eva that the conversation was over, but she couldn't let it end like this. She hurried around the table. "Please hear me out. The fact that Jacob obeyed Bishop right away shows you he respects authority. He—"

"Enough," Louisa interrupted. "We heard you, but there is nothing else for us to do. We said we would talk to Bishop, but that is all we can do. We think you need to start preparing for a Blossom Creek without Jacob Wittmer. He's moved on and you must too."

Eva knew Louisa wasn't trying to hurt her with her harsh words, but they stung nonetheless. Tears filled her eyes, because Eva knew they were right. She needed to prepare for the fact that she would probably never see Jacob again.

A knock on the back door caught them unaware. This early in the morning, with the sun still far off in the east and the bakery closed, the women knew it could be only one person.

"I thought you said he would obey Bishop and stay away as ordered," Rhoda said pointedly to Eva.

Eva could say nothing about why Jacob would come here in the dark of the early morning. Even to her it felt unlike the Jacob she knew.

She backed away into the shadows so as not to be seen and closed her eyes.

Rhoda quietly opened the door and spoke in hushed tones. "Jacob, it's early."

"Forgive me, but I wanted to say goodbye before Eva arrived. Bishop has ordered me to move out, and I have removed my belongings from the apartment. I want to thank you for your hospitality."

"I won't pretend not to know of the ordinance. Bishop informed us. But thank you for coming to say goodbye. Eva's not feeling well today—"

"Eva's sick? She was fine yesterday. Has she seen the doctor?" Concern pitched Jacob's voice up a notch.

Rhoda cast a glance Eva's way before answering. "She's fine. I didn't mean to cause you alarm. You know, I'm beginning to see that Eva was right about you."

Rhoda pushed the door open all the way so Jacob could see Eva. She knew it was obvious she'd been crying. Still Eva stepped forward into the candlelight for Jacob to see.

His face crumpled in anguish. "I did this. I brought this misery to your doorstep. It ends today. I won't be back, Eva. I will honor Bishop's ruling and stay away while I finish up work at the shop. I'll be staying there in the manager's office on the couch. Please know that I will do whatever it takes to fix this for you."

"Will you promise not to leave town without saying goodbye?"

Jacob sighed. "I'll do whatever Bishop asks of me."

"I know you will," Eva said, "because that's the type of man you are."

"I pray I can live up to the virtues you see in me. I want to more than anything."

"Then you will."

"You're going to need to pray for both of us. I think Gött hears your prayers louder than mine."

"I will be praying for both of us." Eva extended her right hand to him, and he took hold of it with both of his. His cold hands shocked her, and more than anything she wanted to invite him in, but to do so would be to ask Jacob to be who he wasn't. Eva had done that once already, and she wouldn't do it again.

Even if that meant this was the last time she would ever see him.

Lighting the candles in the windows each day had never felt so hypocritical. The message of a welcome to weary travelers diminished along with Eva's festive mood. How could she enjoy the Christmas season when she felt like the Bethlehem innkeeper?

Disregard the lights in the windows. They're for show. There's no room for you here. Especially not for you, Jacob.

As if on cue, a white truck pulled up out front. Eva's heart picked up speed, half from fear of breaking Bishop's command and half from wanting to swing the door wide and throw herself into Jacob's arms. Then the driver stepped out and disappointment set in. It was a man but it wasn't Jacob. He just had a similar vehicle to Jacob's, and now he was coming up her walk.

Eva did her best to reset her composure for the approaching customer.

The bell's jingle felt abrasive on her dulled nerves, and her teeth clenched when she forced a smile. "*Güt* morning. Welcome to the Stoltzes' Amish Bakery." Her voice didn't sound like her own. She couldn't hide the fact that it really wasn't a good morning.

The man smiled and nodded but didn't remove his cap. He had a beard and no mustache, but he dressed Englisch. Ex-Amish, perhaps?

Eva didn't tarry to gawk but escaped to her place behind the counter. "How can I help you?" she asked.

"Kaffe. I could really use some this morning. It's been a long night."

Another traveler. "Coming right up." She turned to the urns behind her and began his order. "Do you take milk or sugar or both?"

"Both, please. And I'd love one of your apple spice fry pies. I haven't had one of those in years. My Mamm used to make them when I was a boy."

"You used to be Amish?" Eva asked as she slid his coffee across the counter and opened the case for his treat—the same treat she had left on Jacob's storefront doorstep this morning.

"I left the order when my Fraa died. Too many memories, I suppose. I needed a fresh start."

"I'm sorry for your loss," Eva said as she placed his pastry on a plate.

When she reached for a fork, the customer said, "Don't bother. I'll eat it with my hands in two bites."

"Then allow me to get you a napkin. They're sticky."

"Sticky and good," he said with his mouth full. Taking the cloth from her, he wiped his mouth and hand before drinking from his cup. "So, have you lived here your whole life?"

Eva questioned giving information about herself to a stranger but decided it wasn't too personal. "Ja, my aunts own the bakery, and I work for them."

"Any siblings?"

"Two but one of them . . ." Mentioning Annie's departure would not be right. "Two. I have two siblings," she said firmly.

"It's hard when one leaves the family."

Eva felt a jolt of apprehension. How did he know about Annie leaving? Eva glanced through the swinging doors into the kitchen to see if her aunts were listening. From this vantage point, she could only see Louisa.

The man took another sip of coffee, slurping a bit at the end. "I'm sorry. It looks like I've startled you. I didn't mean to share so much about myself with you so casually. Seeing you run a family-owned business just brought back the hardship of leaving my family behind."

Oh, he's talking about himself. Eva gave a grateful sigh, then admonished herself silently. He was just a man looking for a new start. What was wrong with her? She had always been delighted to be the bearer of fresh bread to her customers, a sign of a new day.

Eva turned to the bread bins and withdrew a long loaf. "I seem to have forgotten my manners. Please take this as a welcome gift to Blossom Creek. Whether this is your final destination or a stop along the way, let this bread represent your fresh start in life."

As she passed it over the counter, the man hesitated. He seemed to question her gift.

"No charge," she stated to clear up any reservations.

"Fresh start in life, you say." The man smiled, but it wasn't a pleasant smile. It was as though he was envisioning a different image than Eva had meant. "I like the way you think." He took the bread and put the empty cup down, then tipped his hat as he headed toward the door. "You have a good day, Eva."

"Thank you. You do the same." Her wish sounded hollow, and she questioned if her heart was in this business anymore. Or perhaps her heart for this job felt empty now that she knew who her heart really desired—and could never have.

The bell jingled as the man exited, and Aunt Louisa pushed through the doors. "Who was that?"

"I have no idea. A traveler passing through. Maybe we'll see him again. Maybe we won't."

"You shouldn't be so forthcoming with information about yourself."

"I didn't tell him anything, other than this was a family-owned business."

"You told him your name. That sounds personal to me."

Eva's eyes widened. "I didn't tell him my name." She rushed to the window. The truck took off down the street, passing Jacob's furniture store and disappearing around the next corner. "I know I didn't tell him my name. How did he know it?"

"If he comes in again, you are to call for us, understand?" Louisa pushed the door wide to go back into the kitchen, shaking her head. "Two ex-Amish travelers in the same month. What are the odds of that?"

11

Eva Stoltz had such a way with fry pies that Jacob felt a bit guilty for devouring them so fast. He had managed to save this one until a few seconds ago when he had told himself he could have one bite. Now he licked the sweet and spicy apple taste from his fingers and vowed to savor it longer next time.

But there wouldn't be a next time.

Jacob headed to his storefront window, his focus back on track. He had to keep Eva safe from Peter. The bakery remained open for another half hour. She was safe.

For now.

He knew her routine well. She would be heading past his store very soon. He reached into his front shirt pocket and withdrew an envelope. In the brief note, he thanked Eva for thinking of him but asked her to stop bringing him baked goods. Jacob didn't want her sneaking out behind her aunts' backs without them knowing her whereabouts. She could get hurt, and they would never know.

Jacob clenched his fists as he remembered how Peter had threatened to harm Eva. He hoped it was an empty threat to make him return to Indiana to fix Peter's reputation. But Jacob couldn't take any chances. He knew that Peter was an abuser and a bully, and even though he didn't have any proof that Peter had pushed Lily, deep down inside he felt that Peter was indeed a murderer.

This letter would end their relationship, whatever that was. They might not be able to see each other, but Eva's gift each day had eased a bit of the hurt. Jacob wondered if he could be satisfied spending the rest of his life with this letter as their only connection. Was it better than nothing?

"I'm heading home," Luke said as he grabbed his coat from the wall rack. "I'll start the new order that came in today first thing in the morning."

"That's fine, Luke."

"Do you need anything else done before I go?"

The letter in Jacob's pocket practically burned through to his skin. Luke could easily pass it on to Eva. "No, I think we're good here." *I'll try again tomorrow.*

"You going to sleep in the office tonight?"

"It looks like that's where I'll be from now on."

"I'll have my wife make you some breakfast tomorrow."

"Please don't. Bishop was very clear that I'm not to have contact with the community. I'm sure that includes accepting breakfast from your family. I'm glad he hasn't told you not to work for me, but that could change. We need to show him we're respecting his order."

"I can't lose this job."

"But you will go if Bishop says so."

Luke frowned and sighed, but at his nod, Jacob knew the young man would be obedient from now on. No more offers of meals to risk his employment. Jacob would have no one in Blossom Creek defying the bishop because of him.

The letter burned again.

"I'll see you in the morning." Luke turned for the door.

"Wait." Jacob reached into his shirt pocket and withdrew the envelope. "Would you mind taking this over to Eva at the bakery before you go home?"

At Luke's hesitancy, Jacob reassured him by saying, "It's the same message I just gave you."

"The fry pies?"

Jacob raised his eyebrows at Luke. "If you noticed, then others did too. Tell her it's best this way. For her."

"I will." Luke reached the door and stopped with his hand on the knob. "You're a good man, Jacob. Whatever happened in your past, it is not who you are now."

"I hope not. Because that man got someone hurt with his decisions."

"You mean the young woman who died?" Luke looked out at the darkening sky instead of at Jacob. The young man wanted to know who he worked for, and he had a right to know.

"I appreciate your loyalty to stay with me, even when you don't know the truth of what happened in my community. You can rest assured, I did not hurt anyone. I was just too late to help them."

"I understand. It makes sense, knowing you now," Luke said, turning to Jacob. "You gave me a job and Sam too. You wanted to help us just as much as we needed the work. And I think you would do just about anything for Eva." He blushed at the meaning of his statement.

But it isn't true.

Eva had asked for his help in finding her sister, and he had turned her down. He'd done it to protect her from trouble with her community and the bishop. But what if he searched for Annie without her knowing?

"Maybe you're right," Jacob responded. "I just might do anything for Eva."

On that note, Luke took his leave.

Jacob went to the sideboard and removed Annie's phone from the top drawer. With the push of a button, he had it powered up. Jacob didn't know if he'd find any information that would lead him to her whereabouts, but checking to see wouldn't hurt anyone.

And if it did?

Visions of giving Eva the best Christmas present filled his mind. She wouldn't want anything else but her sister home for the holiday. And she wouldn't have to know he was involved, just that Annie was home.

Gött, if there is a lead in this phone, I pray You will reveal it to me. And forgive me for disobeying the bishop.

Jacob pulled up Annie's list of contacts. There were more than he thought he'd find, since she was an Amish girl and he had assumed her friends didn't have phones. But there were enough of them to prove he was wrong about that notion. Annie wasn't the only Amish teenager sneaking a phone.

He bypassed the Amish names for anything Englisch. Nothing jumped out at him, so he switched his search to the call log. A number with an Indiana area code stopped his thumb from sliding up the screen. There was no name attached to the number, but this person and Annie had exchanged several calls.

Who did Annie know in Indiana? Family?

Eva had mentioned they had friends in Indiana. Was this the friend? Or was this the man Annie had mentioned she was seeing? Was this the man she had been talking to when he'd overheard her in the parking lot?

Jacob looked at the call time and realized Annie had been talking to this person when Jacob had interrupted her. He racked his brain for what she had called him.

Peter.

A sick feeling compelled Jacob to pick up his own phone. He searched for the list of past callers, one in particular.

The numbers were the same.

Jacob clenched his jaw. Peter Güngerich had been talking to Annie. *How?* How did they know each other? Were Peter and his family the Indiana friends Eva had spoken of? Was that why Peter knew where Jacob was?

Jacob picked up Annie's phone to see how many conversations there had been. When had they started? An old friend would be in here for a long time.

From what Jacob could see, Peter's first call to Annie had been after Jacob arrived in town. Annie's first call to Peter had been the day Jacob caught her on the phone.

The day she left town.

Had she left town with Peter?

Jacob recalled Peter's threat to hurt his girlfriend. The warning had been against Eva, so was convincing Annie to leave town Peter's way of hurting Eva?

If so, he'd succeeded. Jacob couldn't get her pained expression out of his head. He wanted nothing more than to erase it permanently. But there was nothing he could do to help her.

Jacob tossed the phone down on the desk a little too hard and heard it crack. He nearly reached for it to throw it against the wall but jammed his fists into his pockets instead. He needed to remain in control.

His cousin Peter was a mastermind at playing with someone's head. He'd abused Lily and made her believe it was her fault. Wouldn't Peter play mind games with him to try and control him as well? Peter knew exactly how to do it too. Take Annie away from Eva and make Jacob stand by, helpless to do anything to alleviate her pain.

And he'd nearly succeeded.

Jacob had almost run from Blossom Creek, playing right into Peter's plans.

But he'd come back. Peter hadn't succeeded with Plan A. Would he go after Eva personally as Plan B?

A black buggy drove by. A look at the clock told Jacob it was Eva heading home.

Jacob grabbed his coat and keys and ran out to his truck. The engine turned over after a couple of times, and he backed out onto the street.

Going near her was out of the question, but he also couldn't allow her to drive home in the dark alone and unprotected. Not while Peter was out there looking for a way to control him.

Jacob kept his distance from Eva's buggy, its distinctive orange triangle glowing under his headlight beams. The pace nearly stalled his engine, but he kept it idling and moving forward all the way to her family farm.

Eva halted her horse a few feet into the driveway. Jacob stopped his truck in the road to wait until she was safely inside with her family.

She turned her head just so, and he could see her beautiful face in his truck's headlights. He might be the one shining the lights, but Eva was a brighter beacon for him by far.

He wanted nothing more than to jump out and tell her not to worry. He would be here every day, never letting anything happen to her. Peter would never come near her. He wouldn't allow it.

Jacob gave a single wave. "I'll be back tomorrow morning," he whispered. He knew she couldn't hear him, and she had no idea that he would be her shadow from now on.

Eva returned his wave with a small smile and clicked her horse forward. She might not understand why he followed her, but she wouldn't try and stop him.

Eva Stoltz was a smart woman.

"Was that you I heard singing out in the barn?" Aunt Rhoda studied Eva as she tied on her baking apron.

"Maybe." Eva bustled about, her head down to hide the smile threatening to burst forth. She reached for the flour and sugar out of the wooden cabinet and brought them to her prep station.

"Eva Stoltz, look at me," Rhoda ordered.

The box of tin cookie cutters clattered as Eva took them down from the shelf. "I'm sorry. What did you say?" She continued to feign deafness as she rummaged through the box, making more of a racket. "Now, where is my star cutter?"

Aunt Rhoda dropped her rolling pin on her table and came over to Eva. Her presence beside her stilled Eva's searching hand. Rhoda reached in and took the star cutter from the top—proof that Eva had been avoiding her and not really looking carefully.

"You saw Jacob, didn't you?" Rhoda asked knowingly.

Eva shrugged but said, "No, I didn't see him. Not exactly, anyway."

"Then tell me *exactly* how you saw him."

"I said I didn't." Eva turned to face Rhoda as Louisa came into the room, a look of confusion on her face. *Great, now there will be two of them ganging up on me.*

"What's going on? Why such serious faces?" Louisa asked.

"Aunts, I really need to start the gingerbread cookie dough. We'll be so far behind with the Christmas orders if I don't."

Rhoda huffed. "Then we'll be behind, but at least you will still be part of the family. Now, tell me why you are going behind Bishop's back and breaking his order."

Louisa inhaled. "Neeh!"

Eva gave up and placed the box down gently on the table. No work would be done until she told them what had been happening.

Eva hated to, not because she wanted to be rebellious but because it would mean she would be giving up her only time with Jacob, however small it was. After all, she rarely caught a glimpse of him in the dark early mornings and evenings.

But she felt his presence.

His truck's engine behind her the whole way to and from the bakery tendered a sense of intimacy between them without breaking any rules. Knowing he was there conveyed his affection for her.

Her small wave as he drove on past her after she reached her destination was but a small portion of the affection she had for him.

And yet it was enough.

Eva studied her aunts' disapproving faces. They were angry with her, and she hoped she could say the right words to relieve their fears of her presumed waywardness.

"Have you ever been in a situation where you felt cherished from afar?"

Aunt Louisa glanced at her sister for a second, her eyebrows reaching toward her hairline. "Can't say that I have. Are you saying Jacob is *cherishing* you from afar?"

"Yes."

"Just how far?" Louisa said through pursed lips.

"Each morning and evening he comes up behind me in his truck. He stays far back and keeps pace with my buggy. Then after I turn in, he speeds up and drives by. I think he's letting me know that he's still here for me."

"Or he's stalking you," Rhoda quipped.

Eva turned back to her work. "You don't understand. Soon Jacob will leave and—"

Rhoda wrapped an arm around Eva's shoulders. "We do understand. He cares for you, and you care for him. But Bishop has asked Jacob to leave you alone. The fact that he's going against the order doesn't feel right."

Eva swallowed hard. They were words that she didn't want to hear.

"But we're not in contact. Jacob asked me to stop leaving him baked goods, and I have."

"Wait." Louisa came around the table to look Eva in the eyes. "Are you telling me Jacob asked you to follow Bishop's order, but he's not?"

"I suppose."

"Something doesn't add up. When did he start following you?"

"Three days ago, on the way home."

"After he had Luke give you the message?"

At Eva's nod the aunts began a flurry of speculating—everything from an innocent crush to dangerous intentions.

"Stop," Eva cut in. "Jacob would never harm me."

"Right," Louisa said, locking eyes with Rhoda. "He would protect Eva from it, wouldn't you agree, Rhoda?"

Rhoda slowly nodded, her face full of concern. "Protecting Eva would be the only reason he'd break Bishop's orders."

"But I don't need protecting. I'm not in any danger."

"Then explain this Jacob to us. Because if he's willing to disobey Bishop, then he's not the honorable man you think him to be."

Now they were terrifying her. "How can you say that?" Eva whipped around and snatched the ginger and cinnamon from the rack. Baking soda and salt came next. The jars and tins tumbled to the table as she turned to grab the ground cloves. Her vision blurred in her haste to find the gingerbread cookie ingredients.

A soft but firm hand covered her searching one. She froze beneath Aunt Rhoda's touch.

"Tell me about your man," Rhoda said, inches from her side. "The one you know deep inside your heart."

Eva allowed Rhoda's soothing tone to calm her nerves so she could see clearly—not with her eyes but with her heart. "Jacob is a man of integrity and honor."

"And . . . ?"

Eva let a deep breath go. "And you're right. He would obey Bishop's command just as he asked me to unless . . ."

Her aunts held their tongues in unrelenting silence. They would stand here all day if they had to. Eva knew it beyond a doubt.

It was time to face the facts.

"Jacob would only disobey the bishop's order if someone was at risk."

"Not just *any* someone," Louisa said.

"Me," Eva whispered hoarsely. "He must think I am in some sort of danger and need protecting." She stood tall and brave. Now was not the time to cower. "If Jacob believes I'm in danger, then he must have good reason."

Rhoda and Louisa nodded in unison. "*Very* good reason."

12

I'll not see her end up like Lily.

The image of Lily Güngerich's broken neck was never far from retrieval in Jacob's mind, but at some point this week, whenever Jacob closed his eyes, he no longer saw Lily's face in his memory. Now the body belonged to Eva.

But something wasn't adding up.

Jacob hadn't returned to Indiana. He'd stayed and protected Eva from afar. So where was Peter?

Jacob believed Peter would show his face and make good on his threat. The man was used to throwing his weight around. That was the whole reason Lily had run away in the first place. She'd married Peter per her Daed's orders. She was a good and caring wife until the day Peter hit her during one of his tantrums. It was only once, but she knew it would happen again. And so did Jacob.

That was why Jacob had told her to run.

He slumped back on his office couch, trying to rub the tension from his forehead. If only he could go back and handle things differently. An honorable man would have stood by Lily while she went to her family and community. A man of integrity would have spoken up for her to the elders.

A coward would tell someone to run.

But why did I do that? Because I feared for her life? Jacob shook his head. Deep down, where he squelched his guilt for no one ever to see, he forced it out into the light of day. *I told her to run because* I *was afraid to speak up for her.*

Peter's father was the bishop. He ran a tight community. *Strict* was too soft a word to describe the level of authority he had over the village. Even after Lily was found dead and Jacob worked up the nerve to speak to Bishop about Peter's abuse, a part of him was glad that the elder hadn't been home the day he visited the homestead. Only Peter had been there, and he had vehemently denied the accusation.

His word against Jacob's—whom would the community believe? The bishop's son or Jacob Wittmer, Peter Güngerich's shadow?

The two cousins had grown up together, close in age, but that was the end of their similarities. While Peter excelled in everything he did, Jacob struggled and lagged behind. That probably would have been fine if Jacob's father, Moses Wittmer, hadn't been Bishop Güngerich's stepbrother. Moses had come into the family through a second marriage after his father died. His Mamm had married Simon Güngerich, father to Caleb Güngerich and grandfather to Peter. Moses was never fully accepted into the Güngerich family because his mother's order was considered too lenient. What might have been thought of as a good idea to marry turned out to be a strife that lasted long into the next generation and still was going strong. Even to the point of expecting the Wittmer cousin to take the fall for a Güngerich when he caused harm.

Jacob had walked into that vacant farm's silo and had seen Lily dead. He knew in an instant that Peter had something to do with it, and he also knew Peter wouldn't be taking responsibility for it. That was for the Wittmer side of the family only. Jacob would be seen as the villain.

And maybe he was.

Jacob knew leaving would cast more doubt on his innocence in Lily's death, but if what Peter told him the day after she died was true, the police already planned to arrest him. He might not have told Lily to hide out on a vacant farm, and he might not have pushed her from the top of the silo, but by not speaking up for her when she came to him, he might as well have. Running had been his only chance to stay out of jail.

Jacob stood up, but he was uncertain of the direction he should take. All he knew was that he couldn't go on each day waiting for Peter to make his move.

He approached the office desk, now finished and in its rightful place, grabbed the phone, and called Peter's number.

Three rings trilled as Jacob took a deep breath, preparing for Peter to answer—*willing* Peter to answer.

On the fifth ring, he did.

"You're not in Indiana," Peter said with annoyance.

"I'm guessing you aren't either. Where are you?"

"Someone has to watch your girlfriend. She might get hurt. You know how dangerous vacant farms are. Accidents happen all the time."

Jacob bit down hard, clenching his teeth. He took five full seconds before responding. He needed information right now—retribution would come later. "How do you know Annie?" he asked slowly.

"Ah, I see you found her phone. She said she lost it. I wasn't too happy about that. I made her pay."

Jacob closed his eyes, imagining what Peter could mean by that. But at least now he knew the truth. Annie hadn't run away. "So you've moved on from assault to kidnapping. Your Daed must be proud."

"My Daed will never know about this."

"You don't think Annie will tell on you?" *The man is delusional.*

"No, because you will control your girlfriend, or you'll go to jail for murdering her."

Okay, beyond delusional. "And how am I supposed to control her if I can't see her?"

"Once you return to Indiana and tell them Lily jumped, I will allow you to talk to Annie."

Jacob opened his mouth to respond but slowly closed it in silence. *Wait, something isn't adding up.*

Then it hit him. *Peter thinks* Annie *is my girlfriend.*

All this week, Jacob had been protecting Eva, but Peter didn't even know about her. At least not yet. *Please, Gött, keep it that way.* He wondered why Peter thought Annie was the woman he cared for.

The kiss! Or the almost kiss, anyway. Peter must have been watching them in the back lot of the bakery. Jacob had been worried someone had seen them, but he never dreamed it would cause something so sinister.

"I'm not going back to Indiana," Jacob said firmly.

Peter huffed. A rustling followed, then a creaky door opening or closing. It sounded like a wooden barn door.

Within seconds Jacob stopped trying to figure it out because a girl's sobs could be heard through the phone.

Annie.

"Put her on the phone!" Jacob demanded.

"You know what you have to do, or your girl will take a spill just like Lily." The phone went dead.

Jacob redialed the numbers, but it immediately went to voice mail.

More than anything, Jacob wanted to call the sheriff. But growing up Amish, he knew that the plain people kept matters to themselves. Still, this was a kidnapping, and he knew the kidnapper.

But he couldn't lead the police to him.

Not yet, anyway.

Jacob ran out the door to his parked truck. He'd put a map of the state in his glove compartment for his journey here. He slammed his truck door and shook the map open as he reentered the shop. "Luke!" he called.

The young man poked his head around the doorway. "Is everything all right?"

"I need your help. Do you know of any empty barns in the area?" When Peter said something about a vacant farm, Jacob had thought he was reminiscing about his last kill. Could he have been insinuating something about his next?

No, not his next. I won't let him.

Luke came closer, rubbing his hands clean over his pant legs. "Now, let me think. I'm sure we have plenty."

"No, not just a vacant barn but a vacant farm." Jacob's way of thinking took him back to the location of Lily's death. If Peter planned to reenact her death, would he bring Annie to a vacant farm? Or more importantly . . . "A silo. A vacant farm with a silo."

Luke eyed Jacob. "What is this all about?"

"I can't tell you yet, but someone might be in danger." Jacob slapped the open map on one of the tables for sale. "Show me where the vacant farms are."

Luke removed a pencil from his shirt pocket. "The only vacant farms with silos would be the old Fisher farm and this one over on Steeplechase Lane. I don't know who owned it before." He made two *X*'s on areas a good distance apart from each other.

Jacob didn't think he would have enough daylight to search both before the end of the day.

"Why are you looking for a farm with a silo?" said a sweet voice Jacob would know anywhere.

The two men turned in unison.

"Eva, what are you doing here? You shouldn't be here." Jacob heard warning bells sound in his mind. He glanced at Luke, and his breathing picked up at what the young man would do.

Luke backed away, shaking his head and raising his hands. "I wasn't here and I saw nothing." He disappeared through the back door.

The sound of the door slamming echoed through the store.

Silence settled and still neither of them spoke. Jacob drank in every inch of her face, feeling like it had been years since he laid eyes on her. She was even more beautiful than he remembered.

Beautiful—and alive.

A tender smile graced Eva's lips. "I'd tell you to take a picture, but then we'd be in even more trouble."

Jacob snapped out of his stare and looked down at the map, willing himself to calm down. A few deep breaths and he could speak again—but he couldn't say what he wanted to say. *Your sister didn't run away. She was kidnapped because of me. She's in danger and you could be too.* Instead he turned away from her and stared at the now-blurring map. "Go home, Eva. And don't come back."

"I know what you're up to," Eva said to Jacob's back. He hunched over the table, so she walked to the other side to see what he was looking at. A map. A second glance showed two places marked.

"I'm not up to anything." Jacob folded the map before she could determine the marked locations, then pocketed it. "I have to head out while there's daylight. You should go before I do. Someone might see us together." He avoided her eyes.

"You've been protecting me this week," Eva persisted. "Don't deny it. Am I in danger?"

Jacob finally looked at her. He swallowed so hard that she could see the tension in his neck. But his only response was, "No."

Eva retracted, second-guessing herself for a moment. She thought she knew who Jacob was. He would obey Bishop's order, but he would also be truthful with her. *Is he lying?* "You're hiding something from me. Secretiveness is not one of your qualities I prayed for."

"How about protective? Did you pray for that?"

"Is that why you're lying to me? To protect me?"

"I didn't lie to you."

"I'm not in danger then? Because if I'm not, then you've been disobeying Bishop this week by following me. So which is it?"

"For your own safety, go back to the bakery right now."

Eva glanced at the now-empty table. "Why were you studying a map of the area?"

"It's none of your concern, but I was looking at some land. Now please, go."

"Not until you tell me what's going on. Why do you need land? I thought you were leaving soon."

Jacob walked to the door, opened it, and held it wide open for her, his lips sealed tight. Their conversation was over.

Eva withdrew her prayer box from her bag. She willed the box to be the instrument of peace to reconcile them. "I don't know what's caused this divide between us, but I don't think it's only Bishop's order of separation. This is my prayer box that began my petitions to Gött about you."

He stared straight ahead, his hand still on the door. The cold afternoon was turning into an even colder evening. But not nearly as cold as Jacob was acting toward her.

"You really should save your prayers for someone else. I don't deserve them."

"Gött thinks differently about you," she replied. "He put you on my heart to pray for, and He has heard my words. Prayers have no expiration date. Gött will answer them in His time."

When he looked at her, the agony she saw in his eyes nearly made her wish he hadn't. "It's too late, Eva. Trust me when I say this. I've done something horrible, and I can't be saved. Please stop praying for me and go home to your family. They're the ones who need your prayers. Not me."

Eva frowned at his sense of hopelessness. She'd never experienced anything so heavy-laden with despair. Her knees buckled under the weight of anguish she witnessed in Jacob. She wished she could carry whatever burden plagued him.

"Jacob, I will not stop praying for you. Now more than ever, I understand why you were put on my heart. You're lost and broken." Eva's voice cracked at the onslaught of tears. She could feel his pain as though it were her own. "But trust me, you're not forgotten. Gött has a mission, and I am blessed to have a small part in it."

"A mission? What kind of mission?"

"A mission to save." She stepped boldly up to him. With only a foot between them, she lifted her face to his. "Christmas draws near. It is a time of joy for a reason. Jesus came into the world to save us. To save *you*. He came to dwell with us to give us hope, even though we don't deserve it."

Jacob closed his eyes at her words, but whatever gripped him didn't let go. He blocked her out with a simple turn of his head. Conversation over.

Eva couldn't help him. Now it was up to Gött. She placed her prayer box back into her satchel. She would need it for her prayers later. There would be prayers for Jacob, but there would also be prayers for her breaking heart.

As she passed by Jacob, she hoped he would reach for her and stop her. She hoped he would let her help him.

But when the door shut behind her, she had her answer.

Eva kept moving, her heart deeply hurt at his rejection, but something didn't feel right. Her aunts would say she was a glutton for punishment if she went back, and they would be correct. Nothing would come of dragging this conversation out.

Not as long as Jacob believed himself unworthy. Whatever caused him to think this way about himself clearly ate at him. And knowing Jacob, wherever he was headed was probably an attempt to fix his guilt.

Eva positioned herself at the corner of the store and watched the lights go out inside. Jacob was leaving right away.

She shot a glance at his truck. She knew Jacob would never let her go with him. His aloofness inside proved that.

Eva approached the truck and noticed a tarp crumpled up in the bed. Without another thought, she climbed over the tailgate and lifted the heavy material over her. And not a moment too soon.

Heavy boots crunching in the snow grew louder as Jacob neared. The truck shook as the driver's door slammed shut and the engine roared to life.

Eva's body jolted and jostled as the truck backed out onto the street and headed to places unknown.

Now all she had to do was wait to find out what battle Jacob was fighting. What had he done to warrant this life of hopelessness? What guilt consumed him to the point of rejecting prayer for himself? To the point of rejecting her?

Eva felt nauseated, but she didn't know if it was caused by the bumpy ride or the fear of getting answers she might not want to face.

13

Tangerine skies glowed bright beyond a red barn and silo, casting a fiery aura over the dilapidated homestead. The farmhouse stood wide and tall, but the years of neglect overshadowed its vast proportions. The front porch hung on to the structure in only a few areas, there were more shingles on the ground than on the roof, and many of the windows were broken.

Jacob forced his truck through a foot of unplowed snow and knew what that meant. No one had been here in a while.

Probably no one had been here since the last owners departed down the drive, never to return. He wondered what had caused them to leave their home behind. If he had a home like this, he would never leave.

Except he had.

After all, it wasn't the structure that made a place a home. It was the family inside.

Jacob killed the engine and took in the farm. The silo stood about fifty feet behind the barn and reached nearly three times that high into the sky, Jacob figured. A good size for an operating farm. But had the farm failed anyway? Was that why the family walked away?

Stop it. That's not what matters right now.

Jacob opened his door and trudged through the deep snow, scanning the surroundings. The wind caused tufts of snow to swirl over the fields, and the door to the red barn creaked as it swung slowly back and forth. He headed for the barn to search for any occupants, but he didn't think another person was in the vicinity for at least a mile. He couldn't even hear a car's motor. If he hadn't been in a race against the sun, he would have taken a moment to let the peacefulness clear his mind.

Maybe on another day he would return for a different reason, one that didn't involve saving a life.

This place was different from the farm where Lily had been hiding out. Even with the snow around him, the dead of winter hadn't usurped all life from the homestead. The farm Lily had died at had been vacant for so long—longer than Jacob could remember—that it conjured up a feeling of eternal desperation. If Lily hadn't been pushed from the top of the silo and she hadn't jumped to her death, Jacob would say the place had killed her just to continue its misery. He didn't sense misery here, though—only emptiness.

The barn door opened easily. A few pieces of modern machinery told him it hadn't been an Amish family who had abandoned this farm. Images of livestock with room to spare for a workshop played before his eyes. But this emptiness provided no place for someone to hide.

No signs of Annie's presence here. Or anyone else's for that matter.

Jacob continued to the house. He couldn't leave the place without making doubly sure, but Jacob doubted that this was where Peter was keeping Annie. For all he knew, Peter had taken Annie back to Indiana, back to the same farm where Lily had died. This whole search could be a waste of time. He could already be too late.

How would he ever face Eva again?

Simple. He wouldn't.

Eva would have been better off if he'd never graced—or rather, cursed—her town with his presence. She might have some convoluted idea that Gött put him on her heart to pray for, but she didn't understand that his guilt made him too far gone to save. Jesus was born to save people like Eva. Not him.

His boots hit the porch steps, which Jacob was surprised to see were sturdy.

The door was locked. A glance through the cloudy window beside the door revealed an empty living room with a fireplace. He walked down the porch and around the house to the rear door. This knob turned with ease.

Jacob found himself standing in an empty kitchen. Wide-board wood floors extended throughout the room with a thick layer of dust evenly distributed. Not a single footprint broke through any part. It had been months, if not years, since someone had been in this room.

He moved through the spacious room to the next, carefully placing each step until he ascended the stairs and concluded that the previous owners had built a solid house.

From room to room the fine craftsmanship the builder had used both impressed and saddened him. He began to think that perhaps no one had walked away from this home, but instead there hadn't been an heir to take ownership. He swept the dust from the railing as he neared the top. The room to the front of the house glowed with the last rays of the sun. Dust particles floated through the air and flitted away as Jacob made his way to the window.

His truck sat alone down below, the tarp in its bed rippling in the wind. The view of the sunset over the hills cast a beauty over the farm for no one to see but him. The snow glistened with a million crystals in perfect rolling mounds of untouched snow, marred only by his own footprints. Jacob's gaze followed the path his boots had made from his truck—except the footprints led to the bed.

He hadn't gone near the rear of his truck.

Jacob stared at the footprints as far as the view from the window allowed. He hurried to the next room to continue viewing the tracks from another window. From there he could see the whole rear of the farm. The footprints passed the barn and continued to the silo.

Just as he followed them up to the structure, a swatch of red caught his eye as the door to the silo closed.

He felt like he'd been kicked in the gut. It was a color he had seen back in his store. It was the color Eva had been wearing tonight.

Eva.

She was here—he'd brought her here—and she'd just entered the silo.

Jacob ran, his boots pounding down the stairs and echoing through the house. He hit the back door and jumped down the three steps into the deep snow.

"Eva!" Jacob shouted as the snow slowed his attempt to reach her before she saw something she shouldn't see.

Couldn't see.

Visions of Lily's broken body on the floor of the silo assaulted his mind's eye.

Only for Eva, it would be her sister.

Pain ripped through his chest as he struggled to run. Sorrow tore at his heart for what Eva could be facing.

"No, Eva. No."

The silo loomed high above from her place by the door. Darkness stopped Eva from moving forward. The structure had beckoned to Eva when she'd stepped out of Jacob's truck. The silo reminded Eva of someone. Tall, isolated, and empty. *Jacob.*

His emptiness had been clearly evident earlier. He'd lost the part of himself that defined his identity, and there was nothing left of him but a shell. He went about his daily life, trying to make up for something in his past.

But what? What had he done to leave him so empty of joy and filled with guilt instead? Shame drove his every move. He would forever be making up for whatever had happened in Indiana. He would forever be lost and isolated—and empty.

A chill ran up Eva's spine. She suddenly detested this place and wanted out. She moved to lift the latch at the same moment the door was flung open.

"Eva." His arms were around her in an instant. Jacob pressed her against his chest, and she heard his heart pounding frantically. "Please tell me you didn't see anything. Please!" He gripped her shoulders and leaned back to look her in the eyes.

"See what? There's nothing in here. It's empty."

With the door open, some light from the twilight sky cast shadows upon their faces and through the inside of the structure. Jacob glanced over her head, scanning the area around them. Slowly his breathing calmed and he released his grip on her. He touched his forehead to hers. "I was so scared."

"About what? What did you think was in here?" When he didn't respond, Eva touched his cheek. "Talk to me, Jacob. You must know by now I won't judge you. Your past is over."

"It's not, though. That's the problem. And now . . ." He lifted his head, a look of deep sadness on his face. "Now it's hurting you."

"Me? How is your past hurting me?"

His breathing picked up again, and he moved to pull away.

Eva grasped his hands to keep him still. "No more running. I want you to tell me what happened in Indiana. Tell me right now."

"We should go. It's improper for you to be here with me. I can't do this to you."

"You're not doing anything to me. You have nothing to feel shame about. I followed you here. It was my choice. I'm asking you to stay and tell me what happened in Indiana. This is also my choice. Do you trust me?"

"With my life." He frowned. "What's left of it anyway."

Eva met his frown with one of her own. The fact that Jacob would come clean with her in this isolated, empty shell of a structure didn't escape her.

Silence fell between them, but Eva doubted Jacob would turn back now. She allowed him a few moments to pull himself together, and just as she knew he would, he finally revealed his secret to her.

"I have a cousin. His name is Peter Güngerich. He's a few months older than I am. His Daed is the bishop." Jacob swallowed hard and paused.

"I'm listening," she whispered.

Nodding, he continued, "Peter could do no wrong. Which made him a bit of a bully. Some said he would make a good, stern bishop someday but—"

"But not you?"

Jacob shook his head. "He married Lily."

Eva recognized the name of the young woman who'd died.

"She came to me after the wedding and said that Peter hit her. She wanted my help, someone to speak up for her, but instead I told her to run. Peter got word that she was hiding out on a vacant farm, and he told me he planned to go get her and bring her home. I waited until I thought no one would notice me gone and then I snuck out of the house. If only I had left sooner." Jacob's voice cracked, and he squeezed his eyelids shut. "If only I had spoken up for her in the first place."

"What happened?"

"She was dead when I got there. She'd fallen from the top of the silo.

At least that's what Peter said before he ran out. I stayed until the sheriff arrived, not thinking what it might look like. The next day I did what I should have done when Lily came to me. I went to the bishop's house."

"Peter's father."

Jacob nodded. "Only he wasn't there. Peter was. I told him I knew he hit Lily. But it didn't matter. It was my word against his. And his word always weighed more than mine. Then he told me his Daed was meeting with the police to discuss my presence at the vacant farm. He said the sheriff suspected I had more to do with Lily's death than I had told them. Peter said I would go to jail. I said I would tell them he was there too, but he laughed. Again, who would people believe? The son of the bishop or the son of the bishop's unimportant stepbrother?"

Eva ached with the torment in Jacob's voice. He had run from so much more than Lily's death. "You thought running was your only answer, your only way out."

"I thought I could move on, but it's impossible." Jacob locked eyes with Eva. The darkening sky stole the last rays of light. His confession hung over them like the descending shadows, casting them into darkness. "I'm so sorry, Eva. I brought this to your door. You don't deserve this. I don't deserve your kindness or your prayers."

"Shh." Eva touched the tip of her finger to his lips. "None of us deserve Gött's love, but He still sent His Son to earth to die for us. And He still called me to pray for you. His will be done."

"Even if your sister dies because of me?"

Eva flinched as she studied Jacob's guilt-ridden face. "What does Annie have to do with any of this?" She took a step back from Jacob and watched his face crumple at what her distance meant. But the lump forming in her throat wouldn't allow her to give him grace until she heard his answer. *Please, Gött, let it mean nothing. Let it not come between us.*

"Annie didn't run away. Peter took her."

The silo began to spin. With nothing to hold on to, all Eva could do was allow Jacob to take her hand. For a moment, she nearly fell against him to keep herself upright.

But no. As he'd said, he'd brought this to her door.

Eva ripped her hand from his and steadied herself. After a few deep breaths, she processed Jacob's words. "Peter kidnapped her?"

"It looks that way."

"You don't know for sure?"

"I don't know if she went willingly, but I know she needs help now."

"You've known all along that she didn't run away, and you didn't tell me?" Eva's rising voice ricocheted through the silo. She couldn't breathe. She pushed past Jacob to get some air. But even outside, she struggled to fill her lungs.

"Eva, wait! I didn't know. Peter threatened me. He said he would hurt my girl. I thought he meant you. Please stop, Eva. I was afraid he meant you."

Eva followed her footprints in the snow back to the truck. What she planned to do when she reached it, she wasn't sure. How could she return in the truck with him now?

She wondered if she could walk to the nearest house to get help. Or perhaps she could walk home from here. Maybe it wasn't that far, though she had no idea where they were since she'd been riding under the tarp. All she knew was that she had to get away from Jacob.

The realization crippled her, and tears poured from her eyes. Eva's legs gave out, and she fell into the snow. Ice stung her hands as she struggled to push herself up.

Jacob was beside her in an instant. He put his arms around her and scooped her whole body off the ground. Cradled in his arms, she let her head fall into the crook of his neck as the tears flowed.

Eva could feel Jacob lifting one leg at a time through the snow. She was aware that he carried her to the truck, and when they reached the vehicle, she didn't fight him as he gently set her in the cab.

He stood beside her, rubbing her back as she cried. It wasn't until the tears slowed and her cries quieted that she could hear his soothing words. "I will find her, Eva. I promise."

Eva took a few ragged breaths before she formed her words. "You came here because you were looking for Annie?"

Jacob sniffed, and Eva turned to look at him. His eyes glistened with unshed tears. He was hurting too. *But why?* Because he'd caused his cousin Peter to take Annie?

Or because he didn't want to hurt *her*?

Eva knew he would never cause her distress intentionally, but whether either of them wanted to accept it, the direction of their lives had just split in a horrific way. Was that why he was trying not to cry? Was that why more tears spilled from her eyes in a hot flood?

"I came here to look for her because Peter threatened to give her the same death as Lily. I asked Luke where there was a vacant farm, and he showed me this place."

"The map. You marked off this place on the map. I thought you might be looking for a farm to buy. I'm a fool."

"No. You are not a fool. I would give anything to have a home—with you. But—"

"But that's out of the question now. We need to find my sister. That's all that matters." Eva rubbed her frozen hands together, but she couldn't stop the shiver that ran up her arms.

"I'm sorry. Let me get the heat on for you. And then I'm taking you home. I'll find Annie myself."

"I want to help. She's my sister."

"But your bishop has forbidden you to be near me, and your Daed has forbidden you to search for her. No, you're going home, where I know you'll be safe." Jacob jogged around the front of the truck and climbed in. The engine roared to life, and in a short time warm air poured from the vents.

A small smile she couldn't hold back flickered on Eva's lips.

"I'd love to know what is making you smile, so I can do whatever I need to do to cause it again."

She waved a hand to imply it meant nothing. "It's just that I ride in a buggy with no heat every morning and night. The cold doesn't bother me."

"You're dealing with more than cold right now. Shock has a way of chilling you." He turned up the heat.

Eva nodded. "Denki."

Jacob backed out of the driveway and onto the road. He turned on the high beams to expose more of the desolate road. And she'd thought she could walk home from here in the pitch-dark night. *More foolishness.*

They rode along in silence, and she started to recognize their surroundings. As they drew near her home, she found herself pretending that they were on the way to their own homestead in her buggy, anything to forget that Annie was in danger. But they weren't going to a home they shared. They never would.

And then something dawned on her.

"All this week, you've been following me to and from work. You thought Peter was coming for me? That was the danger you were trying to protect me from."

"I thought Peter thought you were my girl."

Eva let the statement slide, leaving it behind them in the dark road. She had wished for Jacob to be hers. He had wished for her to be his.

Neither wish would come true.

"You really didn't know Annie had been kidnapped all this time?" she asked. It was the question that pained her the most.

"I promise you I didn't. I saw her the day she went missing. She—"

"She what? What did she do?" Eva demanded. "I want nothing but honesty from you. I prayed for an honest man. I expect that from you now."

Jacob gripped the steering wheel. "She tried to kiss me."

Eva inhaled and looked out the passenger window, away from him.

"It didn't happen. I scolded her and told her to accept her community before it was too late. I know firsthand what losing your community feels like. I didn't want that for her, but Peter must have seen the interaction and thought that Annie was my girlfriend."

"So he went after her instead of . . ." Eva's voice trailed off as the truth set in.

"Instead of you. And I'm sorry if this makes me a horrible person, but I am so glad he didn't get to you."

Eva glared at him. "Take that back."

"No, I won't. What I will do is find your sister, and I will thank Gött that you are safe. I will thank Him every moment of every day."

Jacob pulled into her family's driveway. He stopped the truck and put it into park. Both sat in silence, facing forward, neither making a move to end their time together.

Her home flickered with gas lantern light, giving off a warm welcome to a lost traveler. Not too long ago, she had prayed for the one sitting beside her. She'd done her best to be the charitable woman her family had raised her to be. But tonight she had failed.

When a moment of doubt came between her and Jacob, she'd snuffed out the proverbial traveler's candle in the window of her heart without a second thought. Had all her prayers been for her own ego, her own wants, and not for answering Gött's call?

Jacob took her hand, pulling her attention away from the lights, and raised it to his lips.

She sat in silence with her thoughts. *Pull away. Don't let him take this direction. It is hopeless.* But she let it happen, watching him kiss her hand gently, almost reverently.

He brought her hand back down to the seat between them and released it, but his tenderness left a hint of reassurance that things were going to work out. *But how?*

"I'm so confused. I want to believe that all will be well. That all hope isn't lost. But I don't trust myself anymore," Eva blurted out before she could try to hide her true feelings. She was so sorry about how she had treated Jacob in the silo.

Jacob nodded. "I understand. I take full responsibility for letting you trust me from the first time we met. You did nothing wrong, and I hope I didn't change your faith in your judgment of others. Keep your beautiful heart for others. Don't ever change, you hear?"

Eva jerked at his words. "Is that supposed to be some type of goodbye? Is that what the kiss on my hand was about?"

"Yes," Jacob admitted, lowering his gaze. "I have another farm to search in the morning. If Annie's not there, I'll go back to Indiana to do Peter's bidding. One way or the other, your sister will be returned safely to you."

"You'd sacrifice yourself for me? After I turned on you at the first sign of trouble?"

"You had every right to. You shouldn't have trusted me to begin with."

Eva fumbled for the door handle. "When I said I don't trust myself, I didn't mean I regret giving my trust so freely. I meant I don't trust my motives of why I do the things I do. I say I want to do Gött's will, but my actions *against* you speak louder than my prayers *for* you." She opened the door and jumped out of his truck before he could respond.

She had doubted him as the man of integrity she had prayed for. The fact that he stayed put to light her path with his headlights only added to her guilt.

14

Annie's bedroom chilled Eva as she opened the door and stepped into its dark shadows. The moonlight shone a beam onto the single bed in the center of the room. A crisply folded star quilt proved Annie was gone. Her sister never made her bed so neatly. It was obviously Mamm's work before she had closed off the room as though Annie never existed.

Eva couldn't blame her mother. *It was the Amish way. If your right eye causes you to sin, pluck it out and cast it out from you.*

Only if Annie had been kidnapped, she had not turned from the Amish way. She hadn't run away at all.

She needed their help.

Eva moved closer to the bed, but something kept her from touching it. Guilt for doubting her sister shamed her. Annie had told her outright that she never had any plans to leave the community, yet Eva had allowed herself to put that out of her mind. *Why did I choose to? What blinded me to seeing the truth?*

Or more accurately, who?

She approached the nightstand and struck a match to light the bedside candle. The single flicker glowed bright from its stand, but the corners of the room remained in darkness. She prayed for Annie's safe return. Then she reached into her satchel and removed her prayer box, lifting it into the warm light. She placed it on Annie's nightstand and opened it.

The single piece of paper brought tears to her eyes. More guilt poured forth. In her selfish wish for Jacob to be hers, she'd lost sight of searching for her real heart's desire.

Aunt Rhoda and Aunt Louisa had given her this prayer box to encourage her to pray to Gött for direction and to find her heart's desire. How quickly she'd concluded that the answer was a man.

Eva pulled out the paper and held it to the light.

I wish for this honorable man to be mine.

Gött had answered that prayer loud and .clear. Jacob Wittmer could never be hers. His past made it nearly impossible, but her sister's kidnapping because of it sealed it as a future that would never be.

An old maid's life loomed ahead. There was nothing Eva could do to stop it. There would never be a family of her own, no children to nurture. And definitely no honorable man to love and grow old with.

Perhaps she should have taken the hint when Daniel left her for someone else. Her simple wish had been spoken out of selfishness, not a need to know Gött's will. So what was her heart's desire, if not for Jacob to belong to her? Daniel's letter had said he hoped someday she would understand. Now she was more confused than ever.

"Eva!" David called from the top of the stairs. Then her little brother burst into the room. "What are you doing in here? What's that you've got in your hand?"

Eva's breath caught—whether out of panic or guilt, she wasn't sure. She pushed the paper at the flame and winced when it caught fire, letting it drop to the tray of the candleholder. The final words, *be mine*, shriveled up and disappeared.

"What was that?" David asked again.

"It was nonsense. Just a silly wish." And gone faster than it was made.

"Daed wants to see you in the barn. You know what that means. Big ouches."

Eva doubted her father would issue a spanking to her at her age. "Did he say for what?"

"Aunt Rhoda brought the buggy and Keepsake back. How'd you get home?"

Her heart plummeted into her stomach and sat there like a boulder. On second thought, she could only hope her punishment would be as simple as a spanking. Going against Bishop's order could cost her so much more. Could cost her everything.

The trek down the stairs turned her feet into lead weights, each step growing heavier and slower.

David stopped at the front door to watch her trudge to the barn, adding his small, sweet voice of encouragement. "I'll say a prayer."

The barn appeared empty when she approached the doorway. Three lit lanterns hung from hooks, and her buggy sat unhitched from Keepsake.

Eva walked to Keepsake's stall and found her horse munching hay. Eva stroked the horse's nose, stopping between the eyes. "Hello, Keepsake. I'm sorry I left you behind. It couldn't be helped."

"You'll have to explain why it couldn't be helped to Bishop in the morning." Her father entered the barn carrying a bundle of hay.

"I can explain," Eva said, dropping her hands to her sides and clenching her fists in the folds of her skirt. "It's about Annie."

"Do not say that name in my home."

Eva had never heard such hostility in her father's voice. She recoiled, but she also didn't miss the grief in his eyes. "You think you lost her, but you didn't. I promise." She rushed forward and stopped in front of him with her arms out. "Please listen to me. Annie was kidnapped."

His forehead creased in concern. It quickly turned to a scowl. "Says who?"

At her hesitation, her father scoffed and sidestepped her for the stalls. "That's what I thought," he said and dropped the hay, continuing with his nightly chores as though she wasn't there.

"Daed?" Eva said quietly. His back tensed at her voice, and she had to push down the tears at her father's aversion to her. "Ann—" She closed her eyes and swallowed hard, almost forgetting about not saying her sister's name. "She needs help. Jacob wouldn't lie about that. He wouldn't lie about anything. That's why this is all happening, because he wouldn't lie for someone. Are you listening to me?"

He moved to another stall with no response.

"What can I do to make you hear me?"

At the door, he said over his shoulder, "Finish up the chores. I told Rhoda you are done at the bakery for the foreseeable future, but you will face Bishop in the morning. He will decide your fate, and if I were you, I'd be asking Gött for some mercy. You have broken an order. The punishment is excommunication. You ask what you can do to make me hear you when you have made it impossible for me to listen. And to trust."

Her father left her standing by the hay, alone. Slowly she dropped to the floor and buried her face in her hands. Just moments ago, she had been saddened, thinking about life as an old maid, but at least she'd known she had what was left of her family.

Tomorrow she could lose even that and be cast out, as the Book of Matthew instructed.

Bright and early, Jacob threw his duffel bag into the cab of his truck and withdrew the map from his back pocket. The paper was folded with the next farm destination on top. He estimated it would take forty-five minutes to get there and another forty-five to leave the county behind.

Snow crunched behind him. Jacob half expected to find Eva standing at the corner of his shop. He wouldn't be pleased with her decision and opened his mouth to say so as he turned to face her.

David stood there instead.

The child's eyes held a fear that put Jacob on full alert. He dropped the map as he knelt to look the boy in the face. "What happened? Tell me."

David's lips quivered, and tears spilled down his cheeks. "I—I wasn't supposed to be listening."

"Who were you listening to?"

"Daed and Eva. After she came home last night, Daed told me to send her to the barn. I didn't know why. I just figured she was about to be scolded. I heard her tell Daed that Annie was kidnapped. Is it true?"

Guilt flooded anew. He'd brought so much grief to this family. "Yes, I'm sorry. Believe me, I am. I'm going to see if I can find her now."

"You have to hurry." David clutched Jacob's forearm.

Jacob looked down at David's hands. They were red and chafed from the icy temperature. "Where are your mittens? It's too cold to be out here like that."

"I forgot them when I snuck out first thing this morning. I had to get to you before it was too late."

"Annie's going to be fine." Jacob hoped it was true. He didn't think Peter would do away with his bargaining piece so soon.

"It's not Annie I'm talking about. It's Eva. She's in trouble."

"With your Daed?"

"With Bishop and the elders. They know she was with you. They're holding a meeting to decide if she is excommuted."

"Excommunicated?" Jacob spoke the word with doubt that it could be true.

"Yeah, that's it. I'm scared. I don't want her to go away."

Jacob covered the boy's hands with his larger ones. "She's not going anywhere. I promise. Once they know the truth, both your sisters will be home for good."

"But Daed *did* know. Eva told him. He didn't believe her."

Jacob had caused more trouble than he'd realized. So much distrust existed now because of him. He stood with his hand on David's back. "Come on. I'll take you to the bakery."

"Eva's not there." David looked up at him as they crossed the street. "Daed forbade her from working there anymore."

Sadness gripped Jacob's heart. Eva had to be fiercely hurting right now, and he could do nothing for her. But he could watch out for her brother and take him to his family. He could also put the child at ease. Eva wouldn't want David to be so afraid.

They reached the sidewalk, and Jacob regarded the bakery. He thought about sending the child on alone so no more trouble was dumped at this family's doorstep. But he had to be sure David was safe.

They walked on side by side. As they stepped up to the front entrance, Jacob stopped.

"Aren't you coming in?" David asked, his hand on the doorknob and one foot on the next step.

"You go on. And stay with your aunts. I'm going to help Eva the best way I can."

"What are you going to do?"

I have to lie. The words hung on his tongue, unwilling to be formed into sounds. "I'm going to pray for Gött's help. Would you pray too?"

David nodded. "But Eva left her prayer box in Annie's room. I saw her burning the paper she kept inside it."

Jacob closed his eyes. Eva had burned her wish. She must believe all hope was lost. Hope for them, hope for her sister—and now hope for her own life.

Jacob promised, "I'm going to bring Annie home. You'll all be back together again soon."

"What about you? Where will you be?"

In jail? "Wherever I have to be to fix this."

The front door opened. "Good morning, gentlemen." Rhoda presented a pleasant tiding for the sake of the child, but her eyes sent a separate message Jacob's way.

"I found this little guy walking the cold streets. Thought you might take him in and warm him up and maybe give him something sweet to take his mind off things today."

Rhoda hesitated at first but nodded. "Go on to the back, David. Aunt Louisa is making sugar cookies. She'll give you some."

David stepped inside, but he looked back at Jacob before following the direction. "I'm glad Eva has you, even if she's not supposed to." With that, he disappeared into the bakery.

Rhoda didn't budge. "I didn't know taking her horse and buggy back would cause my brother to bring Eva before the council."

"It's my fault. All of it."

"Don't be foolish. I watched my niece go to you. She broke the order all on her own. I should have stopped her. I could have, but—well, I suppose my sister and I had seen enough heartache in her life this season. Christmas is a time of joy. We just wanted her to experience a bit of that this year."

"Then I should have never set foot in Blossom Creek."

Rhoda gave a sad chuckle. "More foolishness. Don't you see? When you arrived, joy became possible for her again."

15

The walk up to the one-room schoolhouse stretched for what seemed like a mile-long path. Four men waited inside for Eva: the bishop and three elders. Normally her father would have been one. To avoid conflict, he stayed home.

Or more likely, to avoid her.

Daed had missed breakfast this morning. Eva couldn't remember a time when her father hadn't greeted the day with her before he started his work on the farm and she left for the bakery. His absence spoke louder than if he'd spoken against her at the meeting.

The tip of her right boot hit the first stair. Her fate awaited her just three steps up. Then two. Then one.

Eva took a deep breath at the door and prayed, *Gött, I have sinned against my community. If my punishment is* Meidung, *I will take it, but still, I pray for mercy.*

She opened the wooden double doors and caught a glimpse of the backs of the four men who would decide her future in the community.

A single ladder-back chair sat empty at the front of the room.

Eva swallowed hard and stepped inside. The bang of the doors echoed behind her, and she flinched as though it were the gavel determining her future.

The men did not turn to greet her, so she removed her cloak and bonnet and hung them on one of the empty pegs on the wall. She reached up to touch her white prayer covering and straightened the straps hanging loose down the front of her white apron. She smoothed away nonexistent wrinkles on her Sunday best and pivoted to face the front of the room.

Eva's boots clunked on the wooden floorboards, even though she tried to be invisible with each step. When she reached the chair, she stood by it, her head down, waiting for an invitation to sit.

It didn't come.

Instead Bishop Roy spoke with a bold tone that shredded any last glimmer of hope for mercy. "A community that respects and lives out its district's *Ordnung* generates peace, love, contentment, equality, and unity. It creates a desire for togetherness and fellowship. It binds marriages, and it encourages and enables us to live together, to work together, to worship together, and to commune secluded from the world. State your name."

She cleared her throat. "Eva Stoltz."

"State your sin."

"Disobedience of an order," she whispered.

"We will always have members who will blame the Ordnung when they fall prey to sin."

Eva raised her head. "No, I don't. Please believe me. I love my community."

The men sat in shock at her speaking without permission.

Slowly Bishop stood. "You say you love the community, but obedience is a demonstration to us on whether a member truly loves the church. You see, Eva, one is either in the church or on the outside. There is no happy medium, contrary to the life Jacob Wittmer leads. You may think he has the best of both worlds, but he is without the privilege of the Amish. He is without freedom because he is bound to the outside world. I gave the order for him to separate from our community because I realized there would never be hope for reconciliation."

"Why?" Eva asked without thinking and immediately pressed her lips tightly together to stop any more slips. But her tongue quivered with a demand to know why Jacob didn't deserve a second chance to be brought into the fold of community.

"You dare ask me why, Eva Stoltz. Just this once I will explain it further. Exclusion must apply to all those who live in open sin and those who cause division."

"But Jacob hasn't done any of these things."

"I am not here to try Jacob Wittmer. I am here to decide *your* fate. The outcome of today's assembly will determine if *you* are to be shunned. Your disobedience has caused division. Your aunts have had to choose to inform me or protect you. Your own family has felt the repercussions of your choices as well. Where was your respect to your father and mother when you met with Jacob Wittmer?"

At his silence, Eva took the cue that this question was not rhetorical. Her father's avoidance of her caused her eyes to fill. Blinking back the tears, she composed herself. "Mamm and Daed are heartbroken over Annie. I never meant to cause them more pain. I take full responsibility for breaking the order. There is nothing I can say on my behalf. But I do have a request. Do what you must to me, but I've learned that my sister did not run away. She was kidnapped, but I trust she will be brought home. I beg of you not to shun her when she is. Allow her to stay with my family, so my parents do not lose both of their daughters."

A stony silence fell in the schoolhouse. The elders exchanged glances.

Bishop Roy looked at the men, then back to Eva. "You say your sister was kidnapped. Do you know by whom?"

"Someone from Jacob's old community. He wants Jacob to lie for him, so he took my sister to make him do it. Jacob believes the man is keeping Annie at an abandoned farm nearby. You say Jacob has chosen to live between worlds, but that is not true. He has not chosen this life of isolation, separated from his loved ones. He was never given a choice. He was forced to flee because it was his word against theirs."

"And now you ask us to believe his word about your sister."

"Annie told me that she had no plans to leave the community. She did not go by her own choice," Eva said. "I believe Jacob. And if you can help him find my sister and prove who took her, Jacob would be able to return to his family and community, liberated and free."

"And what about you? Will you willingly take your punishment?"

Eva frowned but gave a single nod.

Bishop cued one of the elders sitting in front of him and returned to his seat.

The elder stood. "Eva Stoltz, it is hereby decided that you are to be shunned for your decision to disobey an order sent down by Blossom Creek's bishop and head of our church. From this moment on, you are cut off."

As soon as Jacob arrived at the second vacant farm, he spotted several sets of tire tracks in the snow. Someone had been here recently.

He drove in and pulled up to the side of the barn, positioning his truck so it would be invisible from the road. He didn't want to alert anyone to his presence right away. Peter might have the upper hand, but Jacob knew the element of surprise would make things a little more even.

Jacob got out of the truck and plodded through the snow, making fresh tracks to the back of the barn. He located a rear door and was relieved to find it unlocked. The interior had barely a gleam of light, but he lifted a flashlight from his pocket and let it guide him deeper inside. Stalls lined the far wall and took up most of the space. The barn at the first farm was more spacious, but this one had more places to hide.

Jacob aimed his light into each darkened stall. One after another came up empty. The double barn doors were next. They were presently closed, but the tire tracks on the dirt floor appeared fresh. Jacob was sure that Peter had been here.

But was he gone for good? And had he taken Annie with him?

Jacob exited the large room, heading down a long hall that led to a closed door. As he got nearer, he noticed a chain on the door. He figured this was the entrance to the silo. The chain gave him hope that this was where Peter had locked Annie up—and that she was still inside.

"His truck's here." A male voice drifted through the thin wall of the hallway, and Jacob could hear footsteps crunching in the snow outside.

Jacob paused in his trek to the silo door and eyed the chain. Could he break into it before the men entered? He rushed forward and grabbed the lock. He twisted it and pulled. Surprised at its strength, he shook the chain and dropped it against the door with a *clunk*. Without a key, it would be useless to try.

A cry from the other side of the door jolted him into trying again. "Annie? Is that you?" Jacob asked in hushed tones.

"Help me!" She banged frantically on the other side of the door. "Shh! Someone's outside."

"Get me out of here! He left me to die!" Annie shrieked as though he hadn't said anything. Her voice rose with growing hysteria. Not that he could blame her. Still, he had to get her to stay calm.

"I promise I'll get you out. You're not going to die. But you must stay quiet. Please, Annie, trust me. I'm here to help you."

"That's what we were told," a voice spoke from behind him.

Jacob whipped around and was surprised to see four older Amish men, with Bishop Roy at the front of the line.

Jacob braced himself for a stern reprimand when the bishop stepped forward.

But instead the bishop asked, "Can you get through the lock?"

Jacob swallowed hard, his mind clicking into gear. "I—I have some cutters in my toolbox in the truck."

"Then get going. That girl has been through enough."

Jacob took off for his truck. He didn't understand how the men knew he or Annie would be here, but on his return with the cutters, he figured it had to be Eva's doing. Of course it was Eva. How could she have stayed silent knowing her sister was in trouble? She wouldn't have kept that from Bishop Roy.

Jacob raced through the door of the barn and back through the hall. The men parted for him so he could latch the cutters onto the chain. One clamp and twist and the lock fell away. Jacob ripped the chain out of the handle and let it fall to the ground in a cascading heap of metal.

As soon as he opened the door Annie burst through it. She collapsed against him, her legs barely holding her up.

Jacob held on tighter to steady her. "It's okay," he murmured soothingly. "You're safe now. You're going home."

"Eva!" Annie wailed.

Jacob handed Annie over to one of the elders. The man's demeanor said it wasn't appropriate for Jacob to hold her, but the man didn't understand the amends Jacob had to make to Annie. After all, this was entirely his fault.

Jacob peered into the silo to see a mat and a propane heater. A water jug lay on its side, empty. "When was the last time Peter was here?" he asked her.

"Eva!" Annie wailed again.

"Annie, answer me. When was he here last?"

Annie forced herself to calm down, but the trembling remained.

"No! You have to listen to me. He's going after Eva. I told him you would never come for me because you didn't love me and he should let me go. That's when he realized you love Eva." Fresh tears spilled from her eyes at the gravity of her statement.

"When did he leave?" Jacob nearly reached for her to shake the answer from her.

"I don't know. Thirty minutes, maybe. He told me he killed a young woman named Lily, and he would kill Eva next. You have to find her!"

Jacob planned to do just that—especially since Peter had now confessed to Lily's murder. He looked to the men. "Where's Eva? I assume you've seen her if you knew to come here."

The men's somber faces gave nothing away.

"I don't understand. Why won't you help me find her?" Jacob demanded. "Why won't you help me save her?"

Bishop replied, "She's been shunned for disobeying my orders. We're not allowed to—"

"Shunned?" Jacob was aghast. "But Eva's never done anything wrong. She's only ever been helpful and encouraging to everyone she meets. Why shun her?"

"She broke an order. It was her choice."

Jacob didn't waste any time trying to figure out what the bishop meant. All that mattered was getting to Eva before Peter did. Desperation tightened its grip on him. "But this is about saving her life."

Bishop Roy studied him, and for a moment Jacob wasn't sure he would speak. Then he cleared his throat and said, "She's at the schoolhouse by the pond."

Jacob sprinted out of the barn and jumped into his truck. He floored it out of the driveway and sped down the road toward darkening skies of doom.

Please, Gött, let it not be a sign.

16

Such a bleak, murky sky for high noon. As the storm blew in over the hills, Eva felt the dread of more than a brewing snowstorm press in. She sat in the buggy, holding the reins as Keepsake took her back to the Stoltz home. No longer could Eva call it her home. She cringed. For how long? Forever?

Tears rolled down Eva's cheeks and pooled at the top of her cape, already drenched from her crying at the schoolhouse. She'd watched the elders leave but couldn't follow suit until her vision cleared enough. Her world as she knew it was over. Shunned from fulfilling work at the bakery, from a lifestyle that offered safety and community, from a family she adored. Eva's life had never felt so dark and directionless. Keepsake could lead the way in the dark of the morning and night, but she doubted the horse could guide her anywhere at this point. There was nowhere to go, no reason to take her anywhere.

Eva knew being shunned would mean silence from her loved ones. They wouldn't be able to partake in a meal with her, would never again be able to welcome her to their table or perhaps even their home. The only solace she had was knowing that Annie would be safe and that the truth would be revealed about Jacob, and his time of being cut off would end. He could finally go home to his family. He could celebrate the birth of the Christ Child, experiencing the forgiveness Gött sent His Son to give. No longer would Jacob's existence be lonely and isolated. This year he would have hope for a better future, one that included a family and a home—even with someone else.

Her heart filled as she imagined his homecoming and then Annie's. Soon her sister would be reunited with the family. *Please, Gött, let it be so. Bring your children home where they belong. They have done nothing wrong and don't deserve to be left out any longer. I am different, as I did bring dishonor to my family and community. I will take my punishment for however long as is necessary. Even if it is forever.*

Eva drove on in a deep, sad silence. Weighted minutes passed, bare moments that depicted the rest of her life as a lonely traveler with nothing but darkness on her horizon.

Oh, how will I bear it? Eva dropped her head in despair. But she pushed the bleakness away to grasp hold of the only hope she could offer herself. *I will go on because I know Jacob and Annie will be where they belong.*

Eva lifted her head to face her new world, but a set of headlights from a rapidly approaching vehicle caught her attention.

The vehicle sped closer, escaping the dark cloud cover in its wake, the driver obviously in a hurry.

But for what? Eva stopped Keepsake and held the reins tight, ignoring the horse's disapproving snort. "Hold up, girl. Something's wrong."

As the vehicle got nearer, she could finally make out that it was a truck. Was it Jacob? Had he not found Annie? Had the elders not discovered the truth about Jacob?

But this truck looked more like the one at the bakery a few days ago that had belonged to the other traveler—the man who'd somehow known her name.

Eva would have relaxed and clicked for Keepsake to start up her clopping again, but the rush of the vehicle paralyzed her. Whether this was Jacob or not, there was still something wrong. When the truck veered into her lane, that feeling turned to instant danger.

The truck was headed straight for her, and Eva had only two choices. Figuring out the identity of the driver wasn't one of them. Eva could either stay still and let the driver plow into Keepsake and her or get the horse out of harm's way.

Eva flicked the reins as hard as she could, yelling, "Go, Keepsake! Move!" She yanked the reins to the right to drive Keepsake off the road, down into the ditch, and away from where the truck could hurt them.

Keepsake whinnied, but she didn't buck at her master's orders. She took the ditch with a leap, and just as her front hooves touched down, the truck reached them. The jolt of the impact and the crunch of splintering wood told Eva she hadn't been fast enough, even though she'd done all she could to save Keepsake and herself.

Seconds flew by as Eva and her horse sailed through the air with the buggy. Keepsake screamed along with her. Eva watched her horse's legs come up as the mare tipped to the right. She never saw Keepsake land, because her world went black faster than any shunning could cause.

Jacob bounded down the steps of the empty one-room schoolhouse. Icy rain and snow pelted his face, but he paid it no mind. The only thing he worried about was finding Eva before Peter did.

His cousin had to be livid that he had taken the wrong sister. All this time Peter had believed he had the upper hand over Jacob, supposedly holding the woman he loved. Now that the truth was out, Peter might take his anger out in a brutal way. Eva wouldn't even know who Peter was. She would have no warning. Jacob could only hope to find her first.

But where would she go?

Eva had just been given the punishment of Meidung. She was cut off from her family, her community, everything and everyone she'd ever known. Going home would feel impossible. Jacob knew firsthand just how impossible. If only he'd had a close family member he could have sought out, like Eva had Rhoda and Louisa.

Her aunts.

Jacob bolted for his truck, slipping a bit on the slick ground, and gunned it for town. Eva had to be there. Her aunts were the two people in her life she could go to in a time like this. They wouldn't turn her away, would they?

"Hang on, Eva, my love. I'm coming," Jacob whispered into the cab of his truck, his words heavy with unspoken promise. Eva would never be shunned by him.

The roads had iced up quickly, forcing him to slow down. He passed two fender benders, and several minutes later the sheriff's car flew by, most likely en route to assist them. Eva was in more danger than people dealing with a few dented cars, and Jacob wished the Amish would set aside their privacy for Eva's sake and seek out the sheriff's help.

Jacob turned the corner and allowed the bakery sign to refocus his determination. At the curb, he jumped out and ran to the front door.

Locked.

Jacob banged on the door repeatedly before he saw the handwritten note. He ripped it from the door, not believing what he was reading. *Closed until further notice.*

Rhoda and Louisa's bakery was their livelihood, and they would never cause such an inconvenience, especially a few days before Christmas, unless there was a devastating situation. Would they close because of Eva's shunning? Life was supposed to go on without Eva. It was part of her punishment to see her family move on without her. If he didn't find her, they just might be doing that forever.

Jacob dropped the note and ran back to his truck. His wheels screeched and skidded as he peeled out onto the street, heading for the Stoltz homestead.

The wiper blades flew back and forth across his windshield, but Jacob could barely make out three feet in front of him. Oncoming headlights warned him of other cars approaching. Otherwise he wouldn't have even known they were out there. The wipers quickly iced up and scraped loudly across the windshield, rendering them useless to push aside the frosty wintry mix. Still Jacob drove on, gripping the wheel so tightly that his hands ached.

But not nearly as much as his heart.

"You won, Peter. You have me in the palm of your hand. I'll do whatever you want me to do. Please don't hurt her."

Jacob saw the flashing lights of the sheriff's cruiser first. Then he saw an overturned buggy and a horse standing a few feet from the road.

Keepsake.

After following Eva day and night, Jacob would recognize her horse anywhere.

"Eva!" He stopped his truck and raced to the other side of the buggy. He slipped down into the ditch and found the sheriff trying to raise the smashed canopy. "Where is she?" Jacob shouted, running to the front. A hand protruded from beneath.

"Help me lift it!" Sheriff Murphy called through the sleet.

Jacob was already there, heaving at the canopy with all his might. It would be a while before Jacob would remember getting the buggy off her, and even then, just bits and pieces. The only thing he would remember for sure was seeing the woman he loved lying still as stone.

After the sheriff and Jacob pulled Eva out and dropped the buggy back to the ground, Jacob looked down and noticed that he was covered in his own blood, his hands sliced from splintered wood pieces. He had never felt a thing except for the terror of seeing her motionless in the snow.

Sheriff Murphy checked for her breathing and a pulse.

Jacob held his breath as he knelt beside her and waited.

"She's alive," the sheriff announced, relief clear in his voice.

Hot tears sprang from Jacob's eyes. He reached for Eva but then remembered the blood on his hands and pulled back, not wanting to soil her.

But when she moaned he forgot all about his cut-up hands. Jacob leaned over her, taking the brunt of the pelting sleet.

Her eyes fluttered open and she looked up at him. No response followed.

"It's me, Jacob," he said, unsure if she had any recollection of him. He regarded the blood on her bonnet. Head injuries could wipe out whole memories. But would it be better for her if she didn't remember him?

The answer was most definitely yes, and he began to move away from her.

Eva clutched his coat and stopped him. "You're hurt," she whispered, still staring at his face.

The blood. He raised his hands to show her, shaking his head. "I'm fine. Don't worry about me."

"But your hands. How will you work if your hands are injured?"

A laugh escaped Jacob's lips. He dropped his forehead to hers. "Oh Eva, haven't you learned yet? It's your concern for me since the day I arrived that has gotten you into so much trouble. I'm not worth it. Stop fretting about me."

Eva frowned, but before she could reply, Sheriff Murphy brought over a heavy wool blanket from his cruiser and draped it over her. "We need to get you out of this icy rain."

She nodded. "I can stand. But I think my arm is broken."

The sheriff turned to Jacob. "Do you want to take Miss Stoltz to the hospital? Or home so her family can decide about her care? Or would you rather I do it?"

Jacob caught Eva staring at him, waiting for his answer. Something told him the question meant much more than simply driving her home. He leaned back and said, "It would be best if you take her. I'll tie the horse to my truck and return her to the farm."

The sheriff lifted Eva into his arms, but she never took her eyes off Jacob. As the three of them reached the cruiser, she asked, "Did the elders find Annie at the vacant farm?"

Jacob had nearly forgotten about her sister. This news he could share with joy. "Yes, your sister is safe, and you'll be reunited soon."

Eva smiled, and Jacob noticed tears in her eyes. "So the elders know you were only trying to help her escape from your cousin?" she continued.

Jacob wasn't sure where she was going with this. He opened the passenger door for Sheriff Murphy to place her on the seat. "I suppose they know. Why?"

"Because now you're free to go home. The elders will vouch for you. I made sure of it, and it was all worth it." Eva turned her head to face forward. She obviously had nothing else to say to him.

But suddenly he had more he wanted to say to her. She made a deal with the elders for *him*? How dare she sacrifice her own freedom for his? His past was never hers to bear. Anger coursed through him, and he reminded himself that none of this was her fault. If it hadn't been for Peter's brutality in the first place, Eva would be safe and part of her community. Whether Peter had set out to hurt her deliberately or not, he was the one who deserved Jacob's wrath.

Jacob slammed the door and kept his mouth shut—for now.

17

The ride to the Stoltzes' farm took a long time with Keepsake in tow. For an Englischer, it might have been painstaking, but for an ex-Amish man, the slow, steady pace brought a sense of peace to Jacob that he hadn't felt in six years.

Did he dare hope his banishment was coming to an end? But if it were so, then Eva had traded her freedom for his, and the idea of her living in exile made him physically ill. He wouldn't allow it. And he definitely wouldn't accept her gift. It wouldn't be right.

When Jacob rolled up to the Stoltzes' house, the sheriff's cruiser was still there, along with an ambulance.

Panic struck Jacob cold. Was Eva hurt worse than she had seemed at the scene?

He wanted to run up to the front door to find out. But the fact that they allowed the sheriff and EMTs into their home would have to be enough for Jacob. He wouldn't intrude on the family's privacy any more than that.

Jacob climbed from the truck and untied Keepsake. He swatted her rump and watched her trot toward the barn. Behind the wheel again, he pulled Annie's cell phone out from the inside pocket of his coat. He hit Peter's number and waited for the man to answer. It took four rings.

"I don't like being kept waiting." Peter's voice sounded more menacing than ever.

"You could have killed her," Jacob replied.

"If I wanted her dead, she would be dead. But that was your last chance. The next time she will be."

"I'm heading to Indiana tonight. I'll be there by morning, and you'll have your story. And then I don't want to ever hear from you again." Jacob hit the end button, but before pocketing the phone, he had a thought. It technically belonged to Annie. Jacob backed the truck out and drove to Bishop Roy's house.

One time when he approached the home, it had been under hospitable circumstances. Jacob didn't think those days would ever happen again.

The bishop answered the door before Jacob reached the front steps. He stepped out from behind the screen, closing the door behind him. "Are you leaving for home? I will keep my promise and vouch for you."

"You should know that Peter hit Eva's buggy tonight. I just came from helping the sheriff return her to her family. Will they help her?"

Bishop nodded. "Her family will care for her well. It is not the Amish way to leave care to others."

"And when she's healed? Will they turn her out?"

Bishop Roy remained silent. Finally he said, "There are ways she can earn out her punishment."

"Earn out? Like the world had to earn Gött's gift of a Savior?"

"Shunning isn't meant to be cruel to those we love. It's to keep peace among the community. I know we have a Savior who forgives and calls us to forgive, but to be lenient in the community brings turmoil to all of us. An order must be followed, or we have chaos."

Jacob sighed, knowing there was nothing he could say to change the outcome for Eva. "I wish I had never come to Blossom Creek."

"But in coming here, you have gained your freedom to return home. I've already sent word to your bishop and elders."

Jacob reached into his coat pocket and withdrew Annie's cell phone. He passed it over to Bishop. "I'm hoping that after everything she's been through, Annie won't feel she needs this anymore and will embrace the Amish way of life with love and respect and obedience—as her sister always has. Whether you see it or not, Eva was only offering the care to me that, as you say, is the Amish way. Good night, sir." He returned to his truck and started the engine.

Bishop Roy remained standing on the porch, phone in hand at his side. Jacob knew the man understood what the loss of Eva would bring to the community. But he also understood how leniency to one member could hurt everyone.

Whatever Bishop Roy decided, it would be a hard decision to make—one Jacob wouldn't be around to see.

With the rain and snow tapering off, the visibility of the road opened up. Indiana was on his horizon while Blossom Creek filled his rearview mirror.

So why did it feel like he was leaving home rather than returning to it?

Eva ran her right hand down the sling Dr. Schneider had placed on her left arm. When she moved, she felt the bandage wrapped around her head press against the wound, and she winced. She'd come away from the crash with only a broken arm and a bump on the head. Sighing, she fell back on her pillow.

Her room darkened as the sun set and cast shadows across her bedspread. The lantern on the nightstand hadn't been lit, and she wondered if she could do it herself. Calling for help didn't seem like a wise decision. Of course, Mamm would come with no complaint, but there would be no affection, no communication. Somehow Eva would rather have had no contact with her family than the strained coexistence she'd experienced since the sheriff had brought her here earlier today. Daed hadn't even stayed to hear the sheriff explain what happened.

Anguish ripped through her heart. Never had she imagined that shunning would feel so wretched. She'd always thought of herself as strong. Now she knew it was only because her family unit had strengthened her. Being cut off really meant being severed from the roots that had given her life. How long could she drift around like the dead leaves of autumn, disconnected and deprived of love?

A floorboard out in the hall creaked.

Eva turned to the sound and waited for someone to enter. She expected it would be her brother sneaking a peek to see if she was awake. Most likely he had been told not to communicate with her, and the idea brought a blur of tears to her eyes. She brushed them away and said, "It's okay to come in. But I understand if you choose not to."

The floor creaked again as someone shuffled to the doorway. Only it wasn't her brother, as she had thought.

"Annie! You're home!" Eva struggled to sit up and cried out at the pain radiating up her injured arm.

"Don't move. I'll come to you." Her sister ran to the bedside and fell to her knees. She reached for Eva's good arm and held her hand, pulling it toward her cheek, which was wet with tears. "I'm so sorry, Eva. I should have listened to you. I shouldn't have run so freely. I have caused so much trouble. And now—now you're shunned because of me."

Eva rolled to her side as gently as she could. "That's not true. I'm shunned because I disobeyed an order from Bishop. I have no one to blame but myself. You mustn't take this on your shoulders. You shouldn't even be talking to me."

"I don't care if I'm caught with you. How can I not blame myself? If I had listened to you, I would never have been kidnapped, and you wouldn't have felt the need to disobey an order to find me."

Eva swallowed hard. "That's only partially true. I also disobeyed because I wanted Jacob Wittmer to be mine. I convinced myself that Gött had sent him to Blossom Creek for that reason. I know now it was to free him from his punishment, so he could go home. That's all."

"Are you sure? Because I have a confession to make." Annie looked down. "I—I tried to—"

"I know. You nearly kissed him. He told me."

Annie shifted her gaze to Eva. "See? That confirms it even more for me. He loves you. I know he does. He didn't want anything to come between you. When he found me at the farm this morning and I told him Peter was going after you, he was so distraught. I could see it in his face. He thought he was going to lose you."

"It doesn't matter now. He'll be reunited with his family for Christmas. And you're safe at home with yours."

"Ours, you mean, right? This is your family too."

"I pray Gött will make it so again. But until then, I accept my burden."

Annie pulled her hand away and reached down into her dress pocket. "I found this in my room." She held up the prayer box.

Eva remembered she had been praying for Annie's return the night before in her bedroom. "I left it there when I was praying for you."

"But where's the paper that was inside? The wish you made that morning when you didn't know I was in the closet, listening to your prayer."

Eva huffed. "No wishes are ever simple. There are always consequences when you attempt to take on Gött's will. I should have never written that wish. I should have prayed for the traveler Gött put on my heart and left it at that. Asking Gött for more was selfish, and my selfishness blinded me to the truth."

"The truth? That you love Jacob?"

"No. To my place in the community. To my obedience to Bishop and Daed."

"But you do love Jacob, don't you?" Annie held the box higher, encouraging her to take it. "There is nothing wrong with making wishes. They're just little petitions to Gött. I made plenty when I was locked up, and all along Gött was sending me someone. Your Jacob."

"He's not *my* Jacob."

Annie frowned and got to her feet. She placed the box on the nightstand. "Jacob Wittmer is your Jacob. Whether you want to see it or not, your wish came true. He will always be your Jacob."

Annie left the room more quietly than she arrived. Or perhaps Eva couldn't hear any other sounds but the roaring of Annie's proclamation through her mind. Her sister was right. Eva might never see Jacob again, but he would always be hers in her heart.

18

A pair of black broadfall trousers lay draped over the footboard of Jacob's childhood bed. He figured Mamm must have made them recently for Daed, as there was no way she could have known her son would come home today. And not only return but return as a free man.

Jacob regarded the Amish clothing waiting for him to reinstate his place in the community. He hadn't expected a warm reception when he pulled up to his childhood home, and he was right not to. He'd sat behind the wheel of his truck for a few moments, summoning up the courage to knock on the door of the white two-story house. When his parents opened the front door, their expressions confirmed there would be no welcome home party.

Still, Bishop Roy had come through, and from what Daed explained, their own bishop was now on the lookout for his son Peter before the police could find him. Jacob understood an attempt would be made to handle Peter quietly within the community. Jacob didn't agree, but saying so only got him shakes of the head. Perhaps Jacob had been gone too long, living among the Englisch, to feel that an Amish punishment for Peter wouldn't be enough. Daed said he would learn the plain ways again, but in Jacob's mind the image of Eva trapped under her buggy demanded justice. The horror on Annie's face when he opened the silo door merited retribution.

Jacob would never be able to prove that Peter pushed Lily, not without Annie's testimony to what Peter had said to her. And if she followed the Amish ways, Annie would never testify. Certainly not in an Englisch court of law. Even if she did, her testimony would only be hearsay. Not enough for a conviction. No, if Jacob planned to bring Peter to justice, he would be on his own.

But because he was home in Indiana due to Eva's sacrifice, Jacob reached for the trousers set out for him. Eva had given him what she thought he wanted. And just a few days ago, she would have been right.

How can I return to the Amish when Eva is cast off? But how can I not when she gave so much for me to be here?

He heard a knock on his door.

"Come in," Jacob called.

His Daed poked his head in from around the edge of the door. Confusion wrinkled his features. "You're not dressed yet? Do they not fit? They should be loose. That is our way. Your jeans are not allowed."

"I know. It's just that I don't feel right about it. I don't expect you to understand, but I don't think I can stay."

As Jacob had expected, his father grew stern. It was why Jacob hadn't gone to him about Lily and Peter in the first place. His father was unapproachable then, and things hadn't changed.

But I am no longer a boy.

Knowing that didn't calm his nerves. "I know you don't want to hear this, but Peter belongs in jail. He murdered Lily, and now he's hurt two more innocent women for no reason except for his own gain."

Daed stepped into the room and closed the door behind him.

Jacob braced himself for the backlash of standing up to his father. "You can't change my mind."

"Why do you think I was going to try?"

Jacob was stunned. "I just figured that Peter is your nephew, his father your stepbrother. Of course you'd want to help them."

"But not my son?"

Jacob sensed that he was broaching new territory with his father. At one time he would have hoped for his Daed to come to his aid over Peter's. But that had never happened. Peter had always been the smart one. The strong one. The right one. Jacob had learned early on his place in the pecking order. He didn't hold out hope for anything different now.

"I know Peter has always been the kind of son you wanted," Jacob admitted, "and I was a disappointment."

"Is this why you never came to me six years ago? Did you think I wouldn't have helped you?"

"It wasn't a hard decision to leave and let the community think the worst of me. It would have been harder to convince you all that Peter was the troublemaker."

"So you let us think it was you instead."

"Did you ever have your doubts?"

"That's not fair," his father retorted. "You never gave me an opportunity to think otherwise."

"I didn't think I should have to."

Silence engulfed the room. More had been said between them in these few minutes than had ever been said while Jacob was growing up. This went so much deeper than the night of Lily's death.

Jacob finally broke the silence. "Can I ask you one question? It's something I've wondered for years."

His Daed gave a single, short nod, but wariness crept into his eyes. Jacob figured he already knew the question.

"Was there a part of you that was glad I left?"

His Daed sighed and dragged a hand down his face, tugging on his gray beard as Jacob remembered him doing so many times when he was deep in thought.

"It's not a difficult question," Jacob said. "I just need a yes or no."

His father reached for the bedpost and took a seat on the edge of the bed. "You think this is an easy question, but there are things you don't know. Things about my brother. We had our own rivalry growing up, and I guess I let it carry over with you and Peter."

"That's not news. The whole community knows that about you two. I'm asking if *you* were glad I left."

"All right, yes, I was glad." His father frowned, and Jacob believed he was being truthful. Even though this also wasn't news.

"I guess this will make things easier if I don't stay. But what will you tell Mamm? She won't understand why I am leaving again."

"We'll tell her the truth. You can't be the man Gött made you to be, because as long as you are here, you will always live in the shadow of someone else."

Jacob studied his father. He no longer saw a severity on his face that instilled fear. Instead he watched sorrow wash over his features. Then the weight of truth seemed to lift from the man's shoulders, relaxing their normal stiffness.

His father stared down at the floor. "Yes, I was glad that you left. But not because I thought less of you. In your leaving, I prayed you would finally be free to become the man you were supposed to be. If you stayed here, I feared you would end up broken." He looked up and met Jacob's gaze. "Like me."

Jacob could hear his own breathing in his ears. Slowly he knelt beside his father. "This is why you never came after me? I went with your blessing?"

"And my prayers. I never stopped praying. I asked Gött to guide your path and to make you into a man of strength and honor and integrity—the man I had always wished to be but traded for the easy way out—being harsh and weak. It doesn't take any skill to yell and demand respect from those smaller than you. I suppose I always feared I wouldn't be a good enough father to earn it."

Jacob nearly told his Daed he was wrong—that of course he would have earned the respect he deserved—but the words wouldn't come.

His father chuckled at what could only be a contorted look on Jacob's face. "Now's not the time for more lies, son." After a few moments he continued, "So, after six years, please tell me that my prayers have been answered. Have you become the man I prayed for?"

"The man of strength, honor, and integrity?"

"That's the one." His lips twisted, and Jacob thought maybe it was a smile.

"Funny you should say this, because there's someone in Ohio who has been praying the same thing for me, word for word. I told her to stop, that I am not that person, but she refused." Jacob cringed. "Even to the point that she has been punished and shunned for seeing more in me than was there."

"She sounds strong . . . and special."

Jacob nodded. "She is also beautiful and kind. But I don't deserve her. I left her to handle everything alone. I haven't been the honorable man you and she prayed for. If I am going to be that man, then I have to go back."

"Ja, son." He took Jacob's hand. His weathered skin was callused and rough on Jacob's.

Does Daed think I can be that man after all?

He squeezed Jacob's hand. "And bring this woman here. I'd love to meet my prayer partner."

Eva sat at her table for one, tucked into the corner of the kitchen. Her family ate at the main table, but hardly a word was spoken among them.

David's fork clattered on his plate, and he quickly righted it. "I'm sorry," he said, a fearful tremble in his voice.

"It's fine," Mamm assured him, but even she sounded unsure.

Eva placed her fork down beside her barely touched food. Her presence caused more tension than there needed to be. She took a deep breath and blurted out what had been on her mind since yesterday. "I think it would be best if I move in with the aunts. My punishment is mine alone, and you shouldn't have to bear it along with me. David shouldn't be on the verge of tears all the time, uncertain of what he can and can't say."

The lack of response spoke volumes. They weren't even allowed to converse with her on matters that would help them. Eva questioned if her aunts would be able to take her in—if they would even want to.

She stood and smoothed her apron with her good arm. "I'll go pack my things." She turned to leave the room.

"You will go nowhere." Her father's deep voice echoed through the room and sent shivers up her spine, rendering her paralyzed. "You think this punishment is only yours to bear, but you are wrong. Your disobedience is a product of my failing as a parent. It is a lesson for us all to learn from so it never happens again. Bishop Roy did not hand this to you lightly. He means for us all to grow in this situation."

"No, Daed, you didn't fail," Eva said. "You always taught me the ways of the Amish and shared your love for the community. You taught me that we love through our obedience. I'm the only one who has forgotten this tenet. I should be the only one to pay."

Annie let out a cry, covering her face with her hands.

Mamm jumped to her feet and put her arm around her daughter's shoulders.

"It's my fault," Annie wailed. "I should be the one to pay."

"No, it's my fault," David said, his lower lip trembling. Tears sprang to his eyes. "I wanted Jacob to love Eva and marry her. I snuck out to find him so he would find her."

Suddenly Mamm let out a giggle that quickly turned into a fit of uncontrollable laughter. She let go of Annie's shoulders to cover her mouth with one hand and hold her waist with the other.

"What is so funny?" Daed demanded.

Mamm regained control enough to say, "Oh Aaron, admit it—we're all guilty. I even had a part in pushing them together by encouraging Eva to take her fry pie to Jacob. A woman gives food to a man she hopes will court her. And it was my idea for her to invite him to Christmas dinner. So, yes, Eva, your father is right. We all must endure this punishment and the pain it brings to us. I, too, was wishing for a wedding before Christmas."

"No, Mamm, please—no more wishes. Gött's will only. And He has made it clear there will be no wedding." Eva turned to retake her seat, the food just as unappetizing as before.

"Knock, knock!" Aunt Rhoda hollered from the back door, opening it at the same time as her announcement.

Aunt Louisa followed her sister. "We brought pie."

No one smiled at the thought of the sweet dessert.

"What a bunch of sourpusses," Louisa said. "It's cherry. And it's still warm. Let me cut you all a piece."

The sisters went to work, whistling as though they didn't have a care in the world—or as if a family wasn't in anguish behind them. Soon plates of pie were set in front of everyone at the main table.

Eva waited with bated breath to see how her aunts would treat her. Would they exclude her from the dessert? Her heart lurched and twisted at the thought. Louisa and Rhoda meant so much to her. She didn't think she could face their rejection, so she stood to take her leave before she had to.

"Wait a minute, Eva," Rhoda called from the window where she peered out into the night. "Company is coming."

"Please don't make me stay," Eva begged. "I can't take any more tonight."

A car door slammed.

Daed asked his sister, "What's going on here?" He went to the kitchen door and opened it.

"You'll see." Rhoda handed Eva her piece of pie and gave her a wink. "Tell him to come in," she called over her shoulder in a cheery, welcoming voice. "We've been waiting for him, and we have pie."

A male voice replied, "That's sounds great, but you wouldn't happen to have some of those apple spice fry pies around, would you?"

19

Sheriff Murphy and one of his deputies entered the Stoltzes' kitchen, and Eva swallowed her disappointment.

"Merry Christmas," the sheriff said. "We're sorry to interrupt your meal."

"Please have a seat at the table," Mamm said to the lawmen. "Let me get you a couple of plates."

"Thank you, but that won't be necessary," Sheriff Murphy responded. "This won't take long. We're here because we think we tracked down the suspect who caused the hit-and-run accident."

Everyone turned to Eva.

Slowly she backed up, scraping the legs of her chair across the wooden floor until one hit an uneven board and thudded to a stop. The pounding of her heart sounded just as loud. She was sure everyone could hear it. "What did you find, Sheriff?"

"It appears to be a piece of the fender of a Chevy truck, the same make as Jacob Wittmer's vehicle. It's been brought to my attention that Mr. Wittmer left town right after dropping your horse off here. Have you heard from him?"

"Jacob didn't do this! I know he didn't. He would never hurt me." Eva's voice cracked with desperation.

"I know that you are—ah, were—a bit partial to Mr. Wittmer," the sheriff told her, "but we did a background check and found that he had gotten himself into trouble in the past. A young woman was—"

"I know about Lily," Eva stated in an attempt to stop the lawman from saying anything more to paint Jacob in a bad light. "He didn't do anything to her. She was dead when he arrived. It was Peter Güngerich who hurt her—who maybe even killed her. Not Jacob."

"Who is Peter Güngerich?" the deputy asked. "Do you have a way to contact him?"

Eva looked at Annie. Her sister's face blanched, but she remained silent.

"Annie, please." Eva stepped toward her sister. "Tell them Peter kidnapped you."

"You will not address your sister." Daed put out a hand to stop her from reaching Annie. "Sit down."

Eva obeyed and took her place apart from her family.

Sheriff Murphy eyed Daed. "Why haven't you reported this?"

"Annie is home safe. We will handle our own matters."

Sheriff Murphy looked to Annie. "Did you see this man your sister speaks of? This Peter Güngerich?"

Annie shook her head and kept it low.

A horse and buggy could be heard creaking down the driveway.

"Oh no." Aunt Rhoda moaned and looked to Aunt Louisa. The women went to the window with crestfallen faces.

"Who's here now?" Daed asked, pushing between them to peer through the glass.

"This is who we thought was coming before," Louisa said, worrying her lower lip.

Boots clunked on the porch steps and across the boards.

Everyone cast glances around the room, waiting for something only the aunts knew about. Their wringing hands said it wasn't going to be good.

Someone rapped on the door, and Daed opened it to reveal Jacob in full Amish garb, holding a straw hat in front of him.

"Good evening, sir. I've come to ask you a question. It's about your daughter Eva."

"What about Eva?" Daed said gruffly.

"May I come in, sir?"

"Neeh, you may not." Daed frowned. "Say what you need to say from where you are."

Jacob looked inside to where the whole family gathered.

Eva sat at her table unable to move. She could see him, but she didn't think he could see her. He looked so handsome and sweet as he scanned the room. She folded her hands on her lap when she really wanted to reach for him. She hadn't thought she would ever see him again, and now he was here on her doorstep.

Asking about me.

Why? What did he want with her?

Sheriff Murphy stepped in front of Jacob. "Mr. Wittmer, I have some questions for you, if you wouldn't mind joining me down at the station."

"Me?" Jacob asked.

Eva could no longer see him, but she could feel his uneasiness across the room. She suddenly remembered why the police had come. He was insinuating Jacob had crashed into her. The words *Run, Jacob* formed silently on her lips.

But clearly Jacob had done enough running.

"Yes," the sheriff continued, "we'll need to see your truck."

"I don't have my truck anymore. I sold it in Indiana and rejoined the Amish. I took a bus back to town and hitched a ride here. What's this all about?"

Sheriff Murphy reached behind his back and removed the handcuffs hanging off his belt.

The clinking of metal brought Eva back to her feet. She knew her own expression mirrored the confusion and fear on Jacob's face. But Jacob quickly swapped his out for a smile, even while the handcuffs were locked over his wrists.

"I tried, Jacob. I did everything I could to give you back your freedom. I have failed."

"No, Eva. You did give me back my freedom. Look at me. I've never been this free in my whole life. You did this. And I've got nothing to hide anymore. I'll go with you, Sheriff. Then, Mr. Stoltz, I'll be back to ask you that question."

"Not if you're in jail," Daed said. He turned around to face Eva. "Pack your bags. You're leaving tonight."

"No, Aaron, she's not." Bishop Roy entered the kitchen.

Gasps echoed around the room. No one had known that the bishop was standing outside on the porch. Had he driven Jacob here?

Bishop retrieved something from his coat pocket and passed it to the sheriff. "This phone will lead you to the man you're looking for. I'm not too knowledgeable about these gadgets, but I know enough that you'll track down your man with it. This Peter Güngerich is in Gött's hands. Not even his family can help him now."

"I'll check it out. Thank you, sir." The sheriff escorted Jacob out. The deputy nodded, then followed and closed the door behind him.

Daed approached the bishop. "What are you saying?"

"I'm saying Eva's punishment has been forgiven. I hadn't looked closely enough at her intentions. She has the Amish heart of charity, and it's stronger than many. I missed it but Gött didn't. He used her to guide one of His lost sheep home. This Christmas Jacob Wittmer has received Gött's gift of freedom to be among the Amish community once again. It is a true Christmas blessing and a reason for much joy." Bishop Roy looked at Eva. "Would you agree?"

Tears spilled from Eva's eyes. "It's all I wanted for him. All I could hope for."

Bishop smiled. "Are you sure there wasn't one more thing you wished for?"

Guilt prompted her to nod. "Forgive me. My intentions were not as charitable as you say. I had prayed for Jacob, but I also wished for him to be mine. I know now that was foolish and selfish and am thankful Gött showed me so. I can assure you that wish is gone forever."

Annie jumped to her feet and placed the prayer box on the table. "No it's not." She opened the lid and revealed a slip of paper. Removing it, she held it up for everyone to read.

I wish for Jacob Wittmer to belong to Eva Stoltz. Forever.

Eva gasped. "Annie, what have you done?"

"When you didn't have enough strength left in you to hope, I hoped for you, sister. You showed me how by all the times you hoped for me in my weakness. Now you don't have to feel guilty, because it was someone else praying for your wish. And I think we should all pray right now for Jacob, because he needs Gött's help tonight."

Bishop reached out to grasp the hands of those closest to him. "I agree with Annie. Who, I might add, is going to be a fine Amish woman in our community. Aaron, you have done well. Your children are a blessing to us all. Now let us pray for our brother Jacob."

Still handcuffed, Jacob sat in Sheriff Murphy's office as the sheriff and his deputy waited for word. Peter's cell phone number was being traced, and they would soon know where he could be found.

"His family is looking for him as well. They might have already

found him and have him back home in Indiana," Jacob offered, even
though he wasn't involved in the conversation between the sheriff
and his deputy. "The Amish like to handle these kinds of things on
their own."

"I understand, but in Blossom Creek, I like to handle these kinds
of things my way," Sheriff Murphy said. "If Güngerich was the one who
hit Miss Stoltz's buggy, I will find him wherever he is and drag him
into my jail cell whether anyone else likes it or not."

"If it had been up to me," Jacob muttered, "I would have seen him
thrown in jail six years ago."

"Because of Lily?" the sheriff asked.

Jacob nodded. "He killed her. I don't have proof, but I know he did."

"What is Güngerich to you?" The deputy cocked his head at
Jacob. "A friend?"

"My cousin. We are a few months apart in age but a world apart
in everything else. I spent my life never measuring up, and then six
years ago, he slipped and showed his true colors. Peter expected me
to cover for him. Or take the blame. Either would have worked for
him, I'm sure. He told me the police thought I was guilty and I would
go to jail for the rest of my life. So I ran, and I've been running ever
since. I know now it was a lie."

"But why track you down here?" the deputy persisted. "He had
you out of the picture."

"I guess some people in the community also saw Peter's true
colors, and that stood in his way of following in his Daed's footsteps
to become the bishop." Jacob leaned back in his seat and sighed. "He
wanted me to come home and clear his name by telling them that Lily
jumped—or that I killed her myself."

"And if you didn't?"

"Then someone else would get hurt."

"And not just someone but the woman you love." Sheriff Murphy's statement silenced Jacob from sharing further. "I'm sorry, but it's obvious to everyone. That's why I didn't understand why you would hurt her. Unless she had rejected you."

Jacob gave a short laugh. "She did. She sent me home to reconcile with my family."

"But you came back as an Amish man again," the deputy said. "Any reason why?"

"I want to try to live up to the man she thinks I am—if she'll have me."

The radio on the sheriff's desk beeped. "Hey, Sheriff, your man was found two counties over. And guess what?"

"No time for guessing games. Just spill it. I've got a man ready to get on with the rest of his life."

"Peter Güngerich has a Chevy truck with a front fender missing. I bet it matches nicely with the one you have in the evidence room."

"Can't wait to reunite them. Did the county sheriff pick him up?"

"They're on their way to Blossom Creek right now. I hear the guy is crying for his father."

Sheriff Murphy shot a raised eyebrow at Jacob.

"That sounds like Peter," Jacob confirmed.

The sheriff got up from his chair and motioned for Jacob to stand. He unlocked the handcuffs, then handed Jacob the cell phone. "I won't be needing this anymore. And I'm sorry I had to suspect you, but I've seen some unlikely criminals in my line of work, and I've learned that things aren't always what they seem."

"No, they're not, Sheriff. There's always more to the story if people want to take the time to really see."

"I think Eva Stoltz is one of those people. Sometimes they see more of us than even we can. Maybe you should trust what she says about you and believe it for yourself. It could change your whole world."

Jacob smiled at him. "That's why I came back. Here I can believe it."

"Merry Christmas." Sheriff Murphy shook Jacob's hand.

"Merry Christmas, Sheriff. I'm glad you will be seeing justice through for Lily."

"You can be sure I'll be in contact with the sheriff in Indiana about Lily," the sheriff added. "I can't make any promises, but I'll do what I can."

As Jacob got a ride back to the Stoltzes' home from the deputy, he felt hopeful that Peter would receive a just punishment for at least one of his crimes. But that was about the only thing he felt hopeful about.

Aaron Stoltz probably had already made it clear to Eva that she would never be allowed to see him again, but no matter what, Jacob wouldn't leave Blossom Creek. He'd come for his bride, and he would wait forever if he had to. She belonged to him, and he belonged to her.

He stepped up onto the porch, then knocked on the door a few times before it flew open.

Eva stood on the other side, and her face lit up when she saw him. "Jacob! You're back already. We've been praying nonstop, but we thought we would need to continue through the night."

"The police have Peter in custody. His truck is missing a front fender. Sheriff Murphy felt sure enough to let me go tonight." Jacob held out the cell phone. "And he returned this."

The phone stayed there between them, neither wanting anything to do with it.

Suddenly Annie reached in and grabbed it from them. "I believe this thing has done enough damage," she said. "But first I need to make one more phone call."

The whole family gathered in the main room as Annie called Sheriff Murphy. She said, "I have a kidnapping to report—and I heard a confession to a murder." She made an appointment to meet with him in the morning.

Annie clicked off, then marched to the front door and opened it. With a quick flick of her wrist, she hurled the phone through the doorway into the dark night. It landed somewhere off in the distance.

Eva let out a gasp. Jacob watched her shock turn into a gleeful smile that crinkled her eyes as she pulled her sister close for a hug. It was clear that Annie was home for good.

Jacob walked up to their father. "Sir?" he began, then suddenly remembered he was still wearing his hat. He removed it and held it in front of him. "I'd like to call on you tomorrow to ask that question."

"No," the stern man replied. "If you have something to say, you can say it now in front of everyone."

All eyes were on him, and Jacob imagined beams of judgment aimed at him. Before he arrived in Blossom Creek, he would have turned tail and run. But his days of running were over. It was time to be courageous, even if he was petrified.

Jacob took a deep breath and blurted out, "I am in love with Eva, and I would like your permission to court her."

"Court her? I believe you have already been doing that behind my back." Eva's father crossed his arms. "Why don't you tell me what you really want?"

Jacob searched Eva's sweet face. He felt his lips form a nervous smile. "What I want is to be the man Eva thinks I am. A man of honor and integrity. I want her to be my Fraa and I her Mann. Sir, I've come here tonight to claim my bride."

He looked at his daughter. "What say you, Eva? Is this what you want?"

Eva inhaled sharply and looked over at her aunts.

Louisa clasped her hands, beaming.

Rhoda nodded and said, "So, what do you say, child?"

Eva faced Jacob and covered one of his hands with her own. "Jacob, Gött brought you to Blossom Creek to become that man of honor and integrity and to claim your bride. I am yours."

Eva's words echoed over and over in his mind. He repeated them to be sure they were correct. "You are mine?"

"Yes, I am yours. I love you."

"And I am yours, Eva Stoltz. Forever and ever. Would you marry me and make me the happiest man in the world?"

"I will marry you, Jacob."

Cheers and claps and laughter erupted from the crowd behind them. Aunt Rhoda barged in and pulled each of them in for a hug. Eva's face pushed into Jacob's shoulder, and he glanced down to see the happy tears glistening in her green eyes. Their faces were inches apart, and their lives would soon close the gap.

Jacob mouthed, "I love you."

Eva gave him a huge smile as tears of joy streamed down her cheeks.

Rhoda shook them with delight, pulling them apart. "A Christmas wedding! We have so much to do. Jacob, komm! I can't think of a better celebration to plan for, can you?"

Jacob allowed himself to be welcomed into the bosom of the Stoltz family and said, "No, I can't think of a more joyous Christmas in my whole life. I was lost but now—" He looked at Eva, her love for him radiating from her beautiful smile.

"Now you belong," Eva finished for him, then mouthed, "to me."

20

Jacob stepped up behind Eva as she cleaned the kitchen after dinner and the festivities. "Merry Christmas, Fraa," he whispered into her ear. His breath tickled her neck and made her giggle.

She whipped around and took his handsome face in her hands. "Merry Christmas, Mann." The side of his cheek was smooth from his last and final shave. She memorized his strong features. Gone would be the solo traveler's bare skin, replaced with the beard of a married man.

But was traveling in her future? Or would they stay in Blossom Creek?

"Why the frown? Aren't you happy?" Jacob covered her hand and brought it down to hold between them.

Her gaze fell to where they were linked. They would be forever linked as Mann and Fraa. "Of course I'm happy." She searched his questioning eyes, doing her best to cover her sadness at the thought of leaving her family. "We'll make a home of our own, won't we? How can I not be happy?"

David dashed into the kitchen. He flew a carved wooden bird high above his head, his attention on the bird rather than where he was headed.

"Whoa!" Jacob said with a laugh as he reached down and scooped David up before he collided with them. "First flight? You might want to keep your eyes in front of you, son."

"Sorry, Jacob. I was coming in to tell you that your gift is waiting for you outside."

"My gift?" Jacob set the boy down and looked at Eva for clarification. She shrugged, having no idea what David meant.

"Daed and Mamm said it was for both of you. Come on!" David grabbed Jacob's hand and yanked hard, leading the way.

Jacob caught Eva's hand to pull her along with him.

The three of them walked into the main room and saw the whole family lined up by the door. Some were standing on the porch outside. Everyone appeared excited.

Eva tugged on Jacob's arm. "Did you know about this?" she asked.

His eyes sparkled. "I did not, Fraa. This is new to me."

They reached the door and halted at the sight beyond the porch steps.

A brand-new family buggy sat waiting for them, with Keepsake harnessed and ready.

Eva was overcome. Tears welled up and spilled down her cheeks so fast she could barely turn around fast enough to drop her head on her father's chest.

He gave her a comforting hug. "Eva, why does this upset you?"

"It doesn't, Daed. I love it." She pulled away from him, sniffling and wiping her eyes. "I love you all so much." *I will miss you all so much.* Eva hid her emotions as best she could. A quick look at Jacob with his full smile told her he had no idea how leaving her home behind would affect her. Until this moment, she hadn't known it herself.

"Well, aren't you going to go out for a ride?" David yelled from behind Mamm's skirts.

Annie and Mamm clapped and laughed, full of delight.

Can't they see our time together is nearing its end?

Jacob wrapped his hand around hers. His touch instantly calmed her nerves. She lifted a small smile to him, to this man who would give her a new home to fill with a lifetime of love together.

"Everything will work out as Gött wills it," he said, his words confirming that her fears were senseless.

"Yes, Jacob. I believe that and I love you."

"Eva Wittmer, would you do me the honor of riding out with me?"

A bubble of laughter erupted from Eva's lips. "Don't be ridiculous! We're not courting. We're already married."

He raised her hand to his lips for a sweet, quick kiss. "May I spend my lifetime courting the woman who gave me my life back? Starting right now. Come with me, Fraa."

Eva searched her family's expectant faces, filled with joy for her. "I am so blessed to have you all. I love you all so much."

"We know. Now go!" Annie said a bit too loudly. She giggled and covered her mouth, the tips of her ears reddening. Eva's sister had embraced her Amish life, but it would take some time before she embraced the quiet life.

Eva gazed up at Jacob. "All right, I accept your offer to ride out."

Jacob tucked her arm into his and led the way down the porch steps and to the left side of the buggy. He helped her up and went around the front, pausing to pat Keepsake's cheek. A moment later he sat beside her, grabbing the reins and clucking for Keepsake to start her drive.

Eva looked back as they rode down the drive. Her family waved like crazy, making her laugh. Quickly the tears formed again, so close to the surface that she whipped around to face the front in silence.

No more tears today. They weren't leaving yet. She would make the best of her final time in Ohio and not worry about her future somewhere else.

"I never knew how much I missed driving a buggy," Jacob said over the clop of Keepsake's hooves and the churning of the wheels on the pavement.

Eva's tight throat didn't allow her to respond. She kept her face diverted to hide her tear-filled eyes, willing them to dry up. Letting Jacob see her cry would make him think she wasn't happy.

"There's something so peaceful, calming, about being behind a horse." His deep voice helped, and she let his words work on her nerves. "It's more than transportation to get somewhere. It's a quiet time for reflection on everyday life, a time to deal with things that might be bothering you. Don't you think?"

Eva looked at Jacob and saw the love on his face—the love for her. She finally let her guard down.

"Talk to me, Eva. It's just you and me and Keepsake."

Eva smiled and glanced Keepsake's way. "I'm so glad she's all right. I did my best to save her."

"I know you did. I could tell when I came on the scene. Even at the expense of your own life." Jacob frowned.

"She's like family. Family means everything to me." Eva dropped her gaze to her hands on her lap. Her fingers intertwined and twisted.

And then one of his hands covered them. So gentle. So loving.

"I would like to take you to Indiana," he said quietly.

She nodded, her throat tight.

The buggy ambled on, cresting a hill. The afternoon sun warmed her face.

"I'm thinking maybe in February, before the spring. Would that be all right with you?"

"I'll go wherever you want, Jacob. I'll live wherever you want."

"That means a great deal to me, Eva. I've decided to buy a farm. I'll keep my shop in Blossom Creek—my team can run it well without me. But for us, I want a farm with a home for our family and a barn big enough to house a workshop too."

They drove on in silence. Jacob took a right at a four-way stop sign and headed over the next hill. The vacant homestead where Jacob had first searched for Annie and where Eva had learned about her sister's kidnapping appeared off in the distance. The red barn glowed bright with the sun shining on its front.

Eva rested her head on Jacob's shoulder. The cadence of the carriage's wheels calmed her as they rolled on through the curvy roads. They would have a lifetime to be together. How different her life had turned out since that afternoon at this farm. She had believed there would never be any hope for them. She was wrong then, and she would be wrong about her future in Indiana.

"I will love my life with you, Jacob, no matter where we are. I will love our farm."

He pulled the buggy to the side of the road and locked the brakes. "It needs a lot of work. We'll have to live with family for a while. I'm thinking two years."

"Two years?" She lifted her head at the absurdity. "An Amish district helps their members. I think you've been gone too long from the community. Surely it won't take two years."

Jacob chuckled and put an arm around her, pulling her close. "Your Daed said the same thing."

Eva gazed out at the vacant homestead and noticed the tall, looming silo. "You see that silo?" she asked.

"Ja."

"When I first saw that towering thing, it made me think of you. All alone and isolated from the house proper. We're married now, and you need to learn the Amish way of life again. Don't be afraid of connecting with your family and letting them help you."

"So, in other words, don't be a silo anymore?" He chuckled deeply.

Eva glanced up at him. "You're laughing at me?"

"Never. But I have a feeling I'm going to have to move that silo closer to the house to make you happy."

"Move that silo?" Eva eyed Jacob with speculation. "Why would you move—?"

A huge smile appeared on his face.

Eva stared at the farm and then back at Jacob.

"Well, Fraa, it's not much to look at right now, but what do you think of your new home?"

Eva tore away from Jacob's grasp and jumped from the wagon. "This is home?" she shouted as she walked up the road. She stopped after ten feet and turned to see Jacob walking toward her. His smile reached his sparkling eyes. She didn't think she'd ever seen him look so happy.

He nodded. "This is home. Our home, Eva. You don't ever have to leave Blossom Creek, and neither do I. But here, it will be a fresh start for both of us."

"Oh Jacob, I love you!" She wrapped her arms around him, and with the sun shining in his eyes, she stood on tiptoe and placed a kiss on her Mann's lips.

"And I love you, Eva. I want to spend the rest of my life giving you your heart's desires."

She leaned in to look him straight in the eyes. "That's sweet, but I already have my heart's desire, and he's standing right in front of me."

Up to this point, we've been doing all the writing. Now it's *your* turn!

Tell us what you think about this book, the characters, the plot, or anything else you'd like to share with us about this series. We can't wait to hear from *you*!

Log on to give us your feedback at:
https://www.surveymonkey.com/r/HeartsOfAmish

Annie's® FICTION